"Save D.A.D."

*A chorus of protests greeted her announcement.
"What? Why? It can't be."*

*Annie raised one hand to quieten the class.
"The board will be having an emergency session
here on Saturday morning to decide what to do."
She mustered a brave smile. "And I'm sure
they'll come up with a strategy to save the
Deerfield Academy of Dance."*

*"See?" Courtney said, tossing a smug look at
Rocky. "I told you so."*

*Rocky ignored Courtney and turned back to
face the gang. "I don't trust the board," she
muttered ominously. "They'll take forever to get
organized -"*

*"And by then the Academy will be gone," Zan
finished.*

*"I think we've got to have our own meeting,"
Gwen declared.*

*McGee nodded. "And we've got to have it
now."*

Scrambled Legs
"Save D.A.D."

Jahnna N. Malcolm

Lions
An Imprint of HarperCollins*Publishers*

To Barbara and Petie
for our wonderful home at Craig's Creek
and to Brian and Cecile for making our time
there so special

First published in America by Scholastic Inc.
First published in Great Britain by Armada in 1989
Published in Lions in 1991
Reissued in 1993

Lions is an imprint of HarperCollins Children's Books,
a division of HarperCollins Publishers Ltd, 77-85 Fulham Palace Road,
Hammersmith, London W6 8JB

Copyright c 1989 by Jahnna Beecham and
Malcolm Hillgartner
ISBN 0 00 693406 4

The author asserts the moral right to be identified as the author of the work.

Printed and bound in Great Britain
by HarperCollins Book Manufacturing Ltd, Glasgow

Chapter One

"It's the spring holiday!"

Gwendolyn Hays pushed open the curtain of the dressing room at the Deerfield Academy of Dance and shouted, "We're free!"

"Geez Louise!" Katie McGee clutched her sweat-shirt to her chest. "Shut the curtain. Do you want the whole world to see us naked?"

Gwen pushed her wire-rimmed glasses up on to her nose and peered at her three friends – McGee, Rocky, and Mary Bubnik. She had caught the girls in various stages of dressing for their ballet class. They stood frozen, holding pieces of clothing in front of them.

"Ooops. Sorry, everybody." Gwen hurriedly

stepped into the dressing room, making sure she pulled the curtain shut behind her. "I guess I got carried away."

"I guess you did," McGee said as she tugged her leotard up over her shoulders.

"Just think of it." Gwen dropped her blue canvas dance bag on the nearest bench and pulled out a bag of M&Ms. She popped a handful of sweets into her mouth and mumbled, "No school for an entire week."

"I like that," Mary Bubnik squealed, clapping her hands together and dropping the blouse she had covering her front. "I just wish it were for a whole year. Then I wouldn't have to take Mrs Callahan's maths class anymore."

"I don't know what you're so excited about." Rocky Garcia stood in the middle of the room, her black leotard halfway up her body and her hands crossed over her chest. She looked ready for a fight. "Spring holiday means Easter, and Easter means – "

"Pink and purple jellybeans!" Gwen cried.

"And Easter egg hunts," McGee added, flipping one of her chestnut plaits over her shoulder.

"And yellow marshmallow chickens!" Gwen continued, her voice getting louder.

"And Easter baskets!" Mary Bubnik hopped up and down, her blonde curls bouncing.

"And solid chocolate bunnies!" Gwen shouted. "And peanut butter eggs with frosting, and – "

"*And* – " Rocky's voice boomed out over the others. "Yucky frilly Easter dresses."

"So?" Mary Bubnik stopped jumping up and down and focused her big blue eyes on Rocky. "What's wrong with Easter dresses?" Getting a new outfit every year and wearing it on Sunday was her favourite part of Easter.

"Nothing. They're fine for other people." Rocky pulled her leotard on with a quick yank. "But have you ever seen me in a dress?"

All three of the girls stared at their friend. Apart from her dance outfit, none of them could remember seeing Rocky dressed in anything but jeans and her red satin jacket with the silver lettering spelling out "Rocky" on the back.

"Come to think of it, no," Gwen said, cocking her head. "Why is that?"

"Because I look stupid," Rocky replied.

"Oh, I'm sure that's not true," Mary Bubnik drawled. "I bet you look great."

"That's what you think." Rocky moved to the dressing table and, grabbing a rubber band, crammed her wild black curly hair into a thick pony tail. "The last time I put on a dress was almost a year ago. My aunt made me this awful bag that was ten sizes too big, and my parents made me wear it

7

anyway. All four of my brothers and every other guy on the base made fun of me."

Rocky's father was a sergeant in the Air Force and her family lived on Curtiss-Dobbs Air Force base just outside Deerfield.

"Well, if you hate it so much," Gwen said, stepping behind the full-length mirror to change into her leotard, "don't wear one."

"Try telling that to my mother," Rocky moaned. "And my dad. He's given strict orders for me to appear in a dress on Easter Saturday."

Sergeant Garcia ran his family like a private army and whatever he said went.

"Maybe if you wore a big hat and sunglasses," Mary Bubnik suggested, "no one would recognize you."

Rocky cocked her head and considered the idea for a moment. "Naw. My brothers would know it was me and tell the whole world."

"Well, look on the bright side," McGee said, pulling at her faded pink tights. She watched in dismay as a ladder travelled from her knee all the way up to her leotard. "Easter's only one day out of the seven we have off."

"Which reminds me," Mary Bubnik said, leaping up and clapping her hands once again. "My very best friend, Kelly Kay Kingston, is coming from Oklahoma to visit for the entire week. I can't wait for all of you to meet her. I think you'll really like her and – " Mary Bubnik's eyes shone as she smiled at her friends, "I know she'll love you."

Mary Bubnik had moved to Deerfield, Ohio when her parents had divorced. At first, it had been really hard for Mary to make friends, and she'd been really homesick for Oklahoma. But when her mother made her audition for a part in *The Nutcracker*, she'd met the gang and she was never lonely again.

"How old is your friend?" McGee asked.

"She's the same age as me – eleven. In fact, our birthdays are only *two* days apart. She lived *two* doors away from us in Oklahoma *and* – " Mary paused dramatically, "Kelly Kay is exactly *two* inches taller than me. Isn't that amazing?"

Gwen stepped out from behind the mirror and quipped, "*Too* amazing." She reached for another handful of M&Ms but caught a glimpse of her reflection in the mirror and winced. The black leotard and pink tights highlighted every lump and bulge in her plump figure. She took a deep breath, sucked in her stomach, and hurried over to the bench, jamming the sweets back into her dance bag.

"Oh!" Mary gasped. "I didn't tell you the best part. Kelly Kay's going to come to our dance classes with us. She's been studying ballet since she was five and is a terrific dancer."

9

Rocky narrowed her eyes at Mary. "She's not a Bunhead, is she?"

Bunhead was their nickname for the snobby girls in their dance class, who wore their hair in tight little buns and thought they were better than everyone else.

"Of course not," Mary Bubnik giggled. "She's one of us."

The girls all went to dance classes for the same reason – their mothers thought it would be good for them. None of them had liked it at first, but ever since they had become friends things had changed. And since they all lived in different parts of Deerfield and went to different schools during the week, their Saturday class was their chance to see each other. Now they thought of the Academy as their unofficial clubhouse.

"That works out perfectly," McGee said as she unfolded a clipping from the newspaper. "You see, this Saturday is the Spring Fest in Deerfield Park. They're sponsoring a huge Easter egg hunt."

"Hardboiled, or chocolate?" Gwen asked.

"I'm sure all kinds," McGee replied. "It's for kids of twelve and under and is a *very* big deal. In fact, it's so big that only teams can enter." McGee's green eyes lit up. She loved anything to do with teams and sports. In the winter she played hockey with the hottest sixth grade team around, the Fairborn Express, and was already in spring training for baseball. "Teams of six," she added meaningfully.

"But there are only five of us," Rocky said, counting their friend Suzannah Reed who hadn't yet arrived at the ballet studio. "Where are we going to get a sixth?"

McGee flashed a big smile and pointed at Mary Bubnik.

"Kelly Kay!" Mary shouted. "McGee, it's perfect. She's almost a member of our gang already."

Suddenly the curtain to the dressing room flew open and a tall, thin girl burst into the room.

"Oh, you guys!" Zan Reed cried. "Something truly terrible is going to happen!"

The girls saw the tragic look on their friend's face and whispered, "What?"

The pretty black girl slumped against the nearest locker and gasped, "They're going to close down the Deerfield Academy of Dance!"

Chapter Two

"They can't close down the Academy," Mary Bubnik cried, beating her fists against the bench in the dressing room. "I was just starting to like ballet." The others stared at her in shock, and she added defiantly, "Well, it's true!"

Rocky turned to Zan. "Are you sure they're closing the whole thing down?"

Zan, who was still slumped against the locker, nodded solemnly. "Positive. That's all anyone's talking about in the front office."

Gwen, who was about to put another M&M in her mouth, paused. "Wait a minute," she said. "Who's the *they* that's closing it down?"

"I'm not sure," Zan said, twirling one strand of her dark, curly hair around her finger.

McGee slipped her feet into her ballet slippers and stood up. "I think we should talk to Miss Delacorte. She'll know what's going on here."

"Good idea." Rocky threw her red satin jacket on over her leotard.

Miss Delacorte was the receptionist for the Academy and their close friend. She had been a prima ballerina in her native Russia and had spent many hours telling them stories about the old days.

"Come on." McGee led the other four girls into the front office where dancers from the company stood clustered in small groups, whispering.

Miss Delacorte, wearing her usual lavender caftan and turban, sat at her desk with her head in her hands.

"She looks just awful," Mary Bubnik said worriedly as they approached their friend.

"Miss Delacorte?" Zan tapped her on the shoulder. "Are you okay?"

The ageing ballerina raised her head and blinked her clear blue eyes at the girls. "To tell you the truth," she said in her Russian accent, "I am feel-ink just rotten."

As she spoke she reached for the box of tissues sitting on top of her desk but her fingers caught the end of the long red scarf wrapped around her neck.

As the girls watched her mistake the scarf for a Kleenex and dab her eyes with the edge of it, they hoped she wouldn't get the urge to blow her nose.

"Here, have a Twinkie." Gwen dug in her bag for the small snack cake that she kept in case of an emergency, and this was certainly an emergency.

Miss Delacorte forced a half-smile. "Thank you, Gwendolyn, but I could not eat a think."

McGee leaned on the desk and whispered, "What's going on around here? Zan says they're closing down the Academy."

Miss Delacorte's eyes filled with tears and she nodded. "It is true. The building will be sold, the ballet company shut down, and my job *kaput*." She reached for the edge of her scarf again. "We will all be out on the street."

The five girls looked at each other awkwardly, trying to think of something to say to comfort their friend. Before any one of them could speak, Miss Delacorte stood up. "My friends, you will have to excuse me. I must go powder my knees."

"I believe it's nose," Gwen corrected.

"Whatever." Miss Delacorte's hands fluttered in the air as she disappeared into the bathroom. The door shut and they heard a low rumbling of voices from the office at the far end of the reception area. Annie Springer, their ballet teacher, seemed to be

14

in conference with Mr Anton and Miss Jo, the directors of the Academy.

Rocky whistled low. "Boy, this is more serious than I thought."

"Do you think they'll cancel our classes?" Mary Bubnik wondered.

"They can't," McGee said logically. "We've already paid for our lessons, we're here, and – " She gestured toward the studio door. "It looks as if everybody's ready to go."

Through the open studio door they could see the rest of their classmates seated on the floor with their attention trained on one person at the front of the room.

Gwen shoved her glasses up on her nose and squinted at the studio. "I can't believe it."

"What?" The rest of the girls gathered around the door.

"It's Courtney. She looks as if she's taken over our class."

Courtney Clay was the head of the Bunheads and the gang's arch enemy. She was extremely pretty and looked like the perfect ballerina. In fact, everything about her was perfect – except her personality.

Rocky cracked her knuckles. "Just because her mother's president of the Academy's board of directors, she thinks she runs the place."

"Board of directors," Zan repeated. "Then she

must know something about why they're closing the Academy. Let's go and listen."

The girls hurried into the studio and took their usual position at the back of the room. Courtney crossed her arms and glared at them until they were seated on the floor.

"As I was saying," she declared with a heavy sigh, "before we were so *rudely* interrupted, my mother says this building is going to be sold and the Ballet Academy doesn't have the money to buy it."

"But who's going to buy it?" one of their classmates asked.

"Some awful developers," Courtney replied, with a toss of her head. "And they're not interested in keeping the building as a ballet school. They want to make apartments out of it."

"Apartments?" Page Tuttle exclaimed. The tall slim blonde was Courtney's best friend. "That's so tacky!"

A small, mousey fourth-grader named Alice Wescott nodded in agreement. "Don't they care about art?"

"The only thing that matters to these people is money," Courtney sniffed, tucking a strand of her hair into her bun. "And lots of it."

Zan raised her hand and asked in her soft voice, "Can't the Academy move to another building?"

Courtney shook her head. "My mother has already looked into that. The ballet company could never find another space as cheap as this one. And they would have to shut down for a year before they could raise enough money to fix up another old building."

"That long?" Mary Bubnik gasped. "I'll forget everything I've learned in a year."

"You'll forget everything you've learned in a day," Page Tuttle scoffed. The girls beside her giggled loudly and Mary Bubnik's ears turned bright red.

"One more crack like that," Rocky growled, brandishing her fist in Page's direction, "and you'll forget your name."

"You don't scare me one bit, Rochelle Garcia," Page retorted.

"Oh, yeah?" Rocky took one step in Page's direction and, with a squeal, the Bunhead darted behind Courtney for protection.

"I can't believe you two," Courtney huffed, putting her hands on her hips. "The Academy is in a complete crisis, and all you can think about is your petty fights."

Rocky, who'd moved back to join the gang, muttered, "Maybe it's not such a crisis, after all."

"What do you mean?" Mary Bubnik asked.

"Well, look on the bright side," Rocky said, motioning for the gang to gather around her. "If there's no Deerfield Academy, then there's no more dance classes."

"And no more sore feet," McGee said, pointing at her toe shoes. The girls had only recently advanced to dancing *en pointe*, and their feet hadn't really adjusted yet.

"And no more lousy leotards," Gwen declared emphatically. She liked seeing her friends every Saturday, but squeezing her pudgy figure into the black bodysuit ranked as the low point of her week.

"Hey, with our Saturdays free," McGee said, her eyes bright with excitement, "we could do lots of fun stuff. Like play soccer, or go on long hikes."

Gwen groaned. "Couldn't we think of something less sweaty, like going for a pizza?"

"Or seeing a film," Rocky added.

"We could have truely great adventures," Zan chimed in. "And maybe solve mysteries together like Tiffany Truenote and her friends."

Zan was an avid fan of the fictional teen detective and had read every one of the books about her.

"But best of all," Rocky declared, narrowing her eyes at Courtney, who was obviously enjoying being the center of attention, "we wouldn't have to put up with the Bunheads!"

"Yea!" McGee cried, punching Rocky on the shoulder.

Mary Bubnik, who had been very quiet for most of their conversation, said, "But aren't y'all forgetting something?"

"Like what?" Gwen demanded, shoving her glasses up onto her nose.

"Like, what if our moms find something else for us to do on Saturdays?"

"You mean ..." McGee swallowed hard. "You mean, what if they sent us back to our old dance classes in our own neighbourhoods?"

Mary Bubnik nodded solemnly.

Rocky shuddered, remembering how awful her lessons had been at the air force base. "That would be terrible."

"We wouldn't see each other anymore," Zan whispered, her deep brown eyes wide with alarm. "Our whole gang would fall apart."

"Wow." Gwen bit her lip worriedly. "I never thought about that."

"Yeah, me neither," McGee said, tugging at one of her plaits.

Rocky folded her arms firmly across her chest. "Well, if I have to take ballet, I want to take it with you guys."

McGee nodded. "It wouldn't be the same with anyone else."

"Then this means that we have to think of a way to save the Academy," Zan declared, her voice low and serious.

"*Us*?" Mary Bubnik looked astonished.

Rocky nodded grimly. "Who else?"

19

"Well, I – I thought that's something grown-ups would do," Mary stammered. "Not fifth and sixth graders."

"We're old enough to handle it," McGee declared, squaring her shoulders.

Just then their teacher entered the room. At nineteen, Annie Springer was already a principal dancer with the ballet company. A worried frown darkened her pretty face.

"I'm sorry for being late, everyone," Annie said, nervously smoothing her hair. "But I've just heard some bad news."

"I already broke the news to the class, Annie," Courtney said importantly. "Since my mother *is* the president of the board and was the first to find out."

"Well, if your mother is so great," Rocky challenged, "why doesn't she *do* something?"

"It's not that simple." Courtney shot her a superior look. "First the board has to have a meeting, then they have to decide how they're going to raise the money, and then they have to appoint a fund-raising committee – "

"That'll take forever." Rocky cut her off with a wave of her hand. "Why doesn't she just *give* the Academy the money?"

"Because she doesn't have it," Courtney snapped.

"A likely story," Rocky grumbled.

"Girls, please, don't argue!" Annie pressed her

fingers to her temples. "You're giving me a head-ache. This has all happened so suddenly, no one has had a chance to do anything about it yet. But I do have to tell you that next week's class will have to be moved to Wednesday afternoon."

A chorus of protests greeted her announcement. "What? Why? It can't be."

"Because — " Annie raised one hand to quiet the class — "the board will be having an emergency session here on Saturday morning to decide what to do." She mustered a brave smile. "And I'm sure they'll come up with a strategy to save the Deerfield Academy of Dance."

"See?" Courtney said, tossing a smug look at Rocky. "I told you so."

Rocky ignored Courtney and turned back to face the gang. "I don't trust the board," she muttered ominously. "They'll take forever to get organized — "

"And by then the Academy will be gone," Zan finished.

"I think we've got to have our own meeting," Gwen declared.

McGee nodded. "And we've got to have it now."

Chapter Three

Immediately after class, the five girls hurried to the tiny restaurant across the street from the Academy for their emergency meeting.

"Hi, Hi!" Gwen called as they trooped into Hi Lo's Pizza and Chinese Food To Go. The little bell over the door tinkled to announce their arrival.

Hi Lo, a small, elderly Chinese man, stood behind the curved counter, wiping drinking glasses with a dish towel. His face rippled into hundreds of tiny wrinkles as he smiled and said, "Greetings and salutations! What's up?"

"Nothing," McGee groaned, hiking herself onto one of the six red leather stools lining the counter.

"In fact," Gwen declared, taking the stool next to McGee, "everything's down, down, down."

Hi studied their glum faces. "This sounds serious."

"It's worse than serious," Mary Bubnik cried.

"It's tragic." Zan rested her chin on her hand and slumped over the counter.

Hi Lo carefully set the glass in his hand down on the counter and said, "Did someone die?"

"Not someone," Rocky corrected, "*some-thing*. The Deerfield Academy of Dance."

Rocky and McGee quickly explained the situation to Hi, who stroked his chin thoughtfully as he listened.

"So you see," Rocky concluded, "the whole Ballet Academy is dead, unless we find a way to keep it alive."

"And that's going to take money," Gwen declared. "*Lots* of it."

Zan suddenly sat up straight. "My school's always doing some kind of project to raise money. Maybe we could do that."

"You mean, like sell lemonade?" Mary Bubnik asked.

"Or have a car wash," McGee added.

"How about a cake sale?" Gwen's eyes lit up. "At my school they sell these huge brownies with chocolate chips and nuts in them. They're delicious!" Just describing them made Gwen's mouth water. "And they cost fifty cents apiece."

"Fifty cents?" Rocky arched an eyebrow. "We'd have to sell a hundred just to make fifty dollars."

"Well, you'd have to wash just as many cars," Gwen shot back, "and baking brownies is a lot easier."

Mary Bubnik crossed her arms on the counter. "How about if we sold lemonade, baked brownies, and washed cars all at the same time?"

"We'd be exhausted," Gwen remarked sourly, "and the Academy would still be broke."

Hi Lo, who'd been listening quietly to their conversation, raised one finger in the air. "May I make a comment?"

The girls turned to him attentively.

"As I see it," Hi began, "you have a very *big* problem."

"Huge is more like it," McGee muttered.

"Well . . ." Hi Lo shrugged. "Big problems need big solutions."

"You mean, we need to come up with something better than just selling things," Zan said.

"I believe so." Hi stepped back from the counter and grinned. "While you girls are thinking, I'll prepare my Hi Lo Super Dooper Easter Special."

"Does it have any secret ingredients?" Mary Bubnik asked cautiously.

24

"Of course." Hi Lo chuckled mysteriously. "But these are all tasty and sweet."

Hi's secret ingredients could be anything from strawberry jam to sesame seeds. Most of the time they were delicious, but every now and then they were just plain weird.

"I don't care what's in it," Gwen declared. "Just so long as it's got something to do with chocolate or ice cream." Without thinking Gwen rubbed her stomach. It hadn't stopped growling since she'd mentioned the fudge brownies from school.

"Just wait and see." Hi pushed open the swinging door leading to the kitchen and disappeared inside. The girls could hear the old man humming to himself as he set about preparing his latest concoction.

"Hi is right," Rocky said, pounding the counter top with her fist. "We need something *really* big this time — bigger than all our cake sales and car washes put together."

"You know," McGee said, adjusting her baseball cap on her head, "my parents are always getting post from organizations that are trying to raise money. They send letters to millions of people all over the country."

"And those people send money because it's for a worthy cause," Gwen chimed in.

"That's a wonderful idea!" Zan exclaimed. "The Academy is the most worthy cause I know."

"What's a million times twenty-five?" Mary Bubnik asked in her soft accent.

All four girls gave her a confused look. "Why?"

"Well, that's how much it would cost to send all those letters for our worthy cause," Mary explained.

"Mary's right," Gwen said. "We need to raise money, not spend it."

"How about leaflets?" Zan suggested. "My mom and dad could print them up at the Art Institute." Her parents taught there and could run them off for free. "Then we could pass them out to people in town."

"What a great idea!" Rocky slapped Zan proudly on the back.

"If we stood on the street corners right at the city center," Zan went on, "we could reach hundreds of people in no time."

McGee snapped her fingers. "If we handed the leaflets out at the Spring Fest on Saturday, we could reach *thousands.*"

"That would be even better," Gwen enthused. "While Courtney's mom and the board are having a meeting to decide to have another meeting – " She rolled her eyes at the ceiling, "we'll be taking *action.*"

"All right!" Rocky shouted. "Now we're getting somewhere."

"Why don't we walk around with big signs on sticks?" Mary Bubnik suggested.

"Picket signs!" Zan chimed in. "We can be protesting about the selling of our school."

"That's a great idea," McGee said. "Then everyone will be sure to notice us at the Spring Fest."

"We need some slogans people won't forget," Gwen said thoughtfully, digging into her dance bag and pulling out another bag of M&Ms, "like, 'Melt in your mouth, not in your hand.'" She popped a few of the sweets into her mouth to tide her over until Hi Lo brought them their specials.

"'It's the real thing,'" Rocky said, pointing to the Coke fountain.

"But we need to sound desperate," Zan cautioned. "We want to get people to care enough to help us."

"A cry for help, like May Day," McGee added. "Or SOS – Save our Ship."

"Or SOS – Save Our School," Mary Bubnik suggested.

"Gwen's eyes lit up suddenly. "How about Save D.A.D.?"

"Do we have to bring our fathers into this?" Rocky asked.

"No, don't you get it?" Gwen explained. "D-A-D – Deerfield Academy of Dance."

"Hey, I like that!" Rocky cried.

"I love it," Mary squealed. "It has a real ring to it."

Hi appeared suddenly, carrying a tray full of huge sundaes, which were in the shape of rabbits. He placed them down in front of the five girls and stepped back. "Presenting Hi Lo's Super Dooper Easter Special for Hungry Thinkers."

Each sundae had a scoop of ice cream for a head and half a banana for each ear. Jelly beans formed the eyes, mouth, and nose, and chocolate syrup had been dribbled over the top of each rabbit's head. Brightly coloured sprinkles clung to the thick syrup.

"Wow, these are the best yet!" Gwen cried, quickly lopping off one of the banana ears with her spoon.

"You really outdid yourself this time, Hi," Rocky said, admiring his handiwork.

"It looks so good, it seems a shame to eat it," Mary Bubnik declared. "I think I'll just stare at mine for a while."

"Don't wait too long," Gwen warned, "or your Easter bunny will become the Easter blob."

Mary looked back down at her sundae. One of the eyes was beginning to droop. "Oh, my, you're right!" She picked up her spoon and dug in. Hi laughed and returned to the kitchen.

"We need to have a meeting," McGee said between mouthfuls, "to make the flyers and posters."

Zan reached into her purse and pulled out a lavender notepad and a pen. "How about Monday afternoon?"

Mary Bubnik shook her head so hard her curls

bounced. "Mom and I are picking up Kelly Kay at the airport."

"What about Tuesday?" Zan asked.

"That's fine with me," Mary Bubnik replied. "Then I can bring Kelly Kay along."

"Sorry, guys," Rocky said, taking another bite of her sundae. "Tuesday's out. That's when my mom's taking me to the BX."

"BX?" McGee repeated. "What's that?"

"The Base Exchange. It's a big department store on base. Things are real cheap there. Tuesday Mom's taking me to shop for my gag-me-with-a-pitchfork Easter dress." She stuck her finger down her throat and grimaced.

"And Wednesday's our ballet class," Zan reminded them.

"And Thursday is bad for us," Gwen and McGee chorused.

"It's our annual Mother-Daughter luncheon," Gwen explained.

McGee nodded glumly. "There's no way we can get out of that."

For the past five years their mothers, who were close friends, had arranged these outings. Gwen and McGee used to loathe them, and each other. Now they just hated the luncheon.

"They make us go to Schaefer's Tea Room," Gwen explained.

"And wear dresses and white gloves," McGee added.

"And, worst of all, eat little plates of lettuce with vinegar on them." Gwen crossed her eyes. "Yuck!"

"Sounds gruesome," Rocky sympathized. "Especially the dress and gloves part." Just mentioning the word "dress' made her shudder.

"So that leaves Friday." Zan set her pen down and folded the lavender pad shut. "I hope that gives us enough time."

"What do you mean?" Rocky asked.

"We'll only have one day to make all of the posters and leaflets," Zan explained, "and plan what we're going to do on Saturday. It seems like an awful lot for one meeting."

"So let's split things up, and do them ahead of time," McGee suggested, licking the last bit of ice cream from her spoon. "Your parents can help you make the flyers, and Gwen and I can make posters at my house."

"Yeah," Rocky agreed. "Then we can spend Friday afternoon practicing chants for our march." She leaped to her feet and shouted, "Push 'em back, push 'em back, waaaaaay back!"

"That's not a chant, that's a cheer," Gwen pointed out. "I thought we were protesting."

Rocky rolled her eyes at the ceiling. "That was just an example." She hopped back up on her stool.

"Don't worry, I'll come up with some really cool chants by Friday."

"Kelly Kay and I can make a big banner," Mary Bubnik said. "She's really good at art, you know. We did a banner for Camp Fire Girls in Oklahoma, and everybody thought it was great. I can't wait until you meet Kelly Kay. I know you'll just love her."

Mary Bubnik clapped her hands together and swept her sundae dish straight into her lap. Melted ice cream and syrup dripped down her tee shirt and trousers in a chocolate-covered avalanche.

Rocky laughed and handed Mary a thick wad of napkins from the dispenser. "Well, if your friend Kelly is half as wacky as you, I'm sure we'll like her."

"Then it's settled," Zan declared, folding her hands on the counter. "We'll each work on our posters at home. Then, on Friday, we'll meet at my house – "

"And review our battle plans to" – Rocky drummed her hands on the counter dramatically – "Save D.A.D.!"

Chapter Four

"There she is!"

Mary Bubnik raced ahead of her mother toward the sea of passengers disembarking from Flight 101 from Oklahoma city. It was Monday and Mary had been counting the minutes until her best friend arrived.

"Kelly Kay!" Mary squeezed through the crowd, knocking her knees against everybody's luggage. She flung her arms open wide at the sight of her friend and shouted, "Hurray! You're here!"

Kelly Kay turned just in time to see Mary trip over a bag of golf clubs and sprawl across the carpet at her feet.

"Oh, Mary, you haven't changed a bit!" Kelly Kay

exclaimed, laughing hysterically. She pulled Mary to her feet and said, "You're still as crazy as ever."

The two girls hugged each other and jumped up and down in a circle. Finally Mary calmed down and said, "Let me take a look at you."

Her friend had grown much taller and thinner. Her long, wavy red hair hung in gentle ripples around her heart-shaped face, which was dusted with a delicate sprinkling of the freckles Mary remembered.

"Wow!" Mary Bubnik exclaimed. "You look wonderful, Kelly Kay. You could be a model for a magazine or TV."

"Oh, Mary, that's not true," Kelly replied, blushing a bright pink. "I'm too tall, my hair looks like a flaming Brillo pad, and I've got awful freckles."

At that moment Mrs Bubnik caught up with the two girls and gave Kelly a big warm hug. Then she held the girl at arm's length. "Look at you, Kelly Kay. Now haven't you grown so tall and pretty!"

"See? I told you," Mary said, nudging her friend with her elbow.

"Will you stop?" Kelly Kay giggled and nudged her back.

"I was just telling her that, Mom," Mary said excitedly. "Isn't she just the most gorgeous girl you ever did see?"

"Yes, besides you, sweetheart," Mrs Bubnik

replied, reaching round to give Mary a squeeze with her free hand. "Well, Kelly Kay, let's go and get your suitcases from the baggage claim."

"You can't miss them," Kelly said. "All my luggage is purple."

"I can't believe it!" Mary exclaimed. "Is purple still your favourite colour? I've changed mine three times since I left Oklahoma."

"What is it now?" Kelly asked as they moved closer to the conveyor belt.

"Hmmm." Mary cocked her head thoughtfully for a minute. She couldn't remember if her current favourite colour was pink or blue. Then her face lit up. "I always think of purple when I'm with you," she declared. "So for the whole time you're here — it will be purple!"

Mary Bubnik was grinning so hard her face hurt. It had been almost six months since the two had last seen each other. But it felt like no time had passed. They were still exactly the same.

Kelly's purple nylon bags rolled by on the conveyor belt, and the girls lugged them out to the waiting car.

"You've still got this old car?" Kelly Kay exclaimed as she tossed her bags into the trunk. "I can't believe it's still running."

"Neither can we," Mrs Bubnik said dryly.

Mary patted the fender of the old green Volvo

affectionately. "Mr Toad is our friend, isn't he, Mom? We'd never be able to part with him."

"That's right," her mother agreed. "He's practically a member of the family."

The girls clambered into the back seat and huddled together so they could catch up on old times.

"So tell me all about Oklahoma City," Mary Bubnik said breathlessly. "What's been going on in school since I left?"

"Well, it's kind of the same, you know" Kelly Kay replied. "The same popular crowd with jerky Janice Edmonds running everything."

They both made a face like they'd eaten a lemon.

"Only it's worse," Kelly went on, "'cause now she's class president."

"What?" Mary Bubnik cried indignantly. "I can't believe it!"

"Me neither." Kelly lowered her voice to a whisper. "We think the ballot boxes were stuffed because we couldn't imagine that so many kids liked Janice enough to vote for her."

"That would be just like her to do that," Mary sniffed.

Suddenly Kelly giggled. "Remember when we put the sneezing powder in Janice's desk?"

"Oh, do I ever!" Mary squealed. "And remember

when I was lunch monitor and I accidentally dropped an entire jelly salad on her head?"

"Mary, that's terrible!" Mrs Bubnik interrupted as the girls laughed hysterically. "I had no idea you did that!" She tried to sound stern, but Mary could hear her mother chuckling over the incident in spite of herself.

"Oh, Mom, it was awful!" Mary said between giggles. "I had to spend a whole hour in the principal's office."

"Remember the time we played gypsies in the school play," Kelly Kay went on, "and your veils got stuck in the cardboard wagon wheel, and we thought you were going to get run over?"

"That was so much fun," Mary said, leaning her head back against the seat. "Especially when B. J. Macintosh rescued me."

"Yeah, except he ripped your dress," Kelly added.

"I think that was one of the most embarrassing moments of my entire life." Mary covered her face with her hands. "There I was, standing in front of everybody in my underwear."

"But the crowd loved you," Kelly insisted, her eyes shining. "You got the most applause at the curtain call."

Mary shook her head slowly and sighed, "Boy, that all seems years ago, doesn't it?"

Kelly Kay nodded. "It sure does."

They sat there quietly for a moment. "So tell me what's new with you." She smiled expectantly.

Kelly Kay faced forward and shrugged. "There's not much to tell. You know, the same old stuff."

"Are you still in dance school?"

"Of course," Kelly replied. "And Miss Lynn is just the same as ever."

Mary giggled. "Still talking about that beauty contest she didn't win?"

"That's right," Kelly Kay said with a grin. "If she hadn't dropped the baton in her twirling-on-toes number, she swears she would have been first runner-up in the Miss Oklahoma pageant."

"She probably would have," Mary agreed. "Miss Lynn's so pretty and, let's face it, her talent was unique."

"Weird, is more like it," Kelly Kay remarked. "Well, she's phased out the baton twirling, and is focusing strictly on ballet." She looked up shyly. "In fact, she got some of us to do a recital for the Kiwanis Club."

"You're kidding!" Mary Bubnik sat up straight. "You must be really good!"

Kelly Kay blushed so hard, her freckles turned red. "Well, I've been taking a few more classes and I think I've really improved."

Mary hugged her proudly. "I can't wait to take you to my dance class at the Academy. My friends will be so impressed."

37

"Friends?" Kelly Kay carefully tucked her fluffy red hair behind one ear. "At school?"

"No, in my ballet class. I'm sure I wrote to you about them. They're all the greatest!"

"Oh, yes." Kelly's voice was subdued. "Now I remember."

Mary giggled and put her hand on Kelly Kay's arm. "Not as great as you, of course. But I know you'll really like them."

Mrs Bubnik, who'd been listening from the front seat, agreed. "These girls are really very different. But they've been a lifesaver for Mary."

"That's nice," Kelly said with a tight smile. "But did you really need saving?"

Mary Bubnik nodded emphatically. "I had a really hard time when we first moved here. Nobody at school wanted to meet me, I couldn't make any friends in our neighbourhood, no matter how hard I tried – and then I met the gang."

"Gang?" Kelly Kay looked alarmed. "Are you a club or something? How many are there?"

"Five, counting me," Mary replied, "and we're like this." She held up her hand with her fingers crossed.

"Oh."

"They're nothing like the kids in Oklahoma." Mary Bubnik shook her head and laughed. "Gwen is really funny and McGee can play just about every sport. You'll think Rocky is kind of tough, but inside

38

she's just an old softie. Oh, and Zan is so smart and interesting."

"Really?" Kelly asked without looking at her.

"Yeah," Mary nodded, her head and her curls bounced. "We've had some great adventures together."

"In Deerfield?" Kelly sat forward. "Is there *that* much to do here?"

"Are you kidding?" Mary Bubnik said. "There's tons of things. It's much more exciting than Oklahoma ever was."

Kelly Kay didn't say anything. She just looked out the window.

"Anyway, it's just perfect you came when you did," Mary chattered on. "We're in real trouble."

"Yeah?" Kelly Kay perked up slightly.

Mary quickly told both Kelly and her mother about the building crisis. "So you see, if the Academy closes, it could mean the end of our friendship."

"Gee, that's too bad." Kelly Kay dug in her purse for a compact and lip gloss. "But I'm sure you'll make other friends."

"Not like these guys," Mary insisted. "You'll see."

Kelly Kay quietly examined her face in the tiny mirror and said nothing.

"Anyway, here's the plan," Mary announced, ticking the events off on her fingers. "On Wednesday we go to class at the Academy. On Friday we get our signs together and practice our chants with the gang. Then on Saturday we march in the morning at the Spring Fest, and hunt for Easter eggs in the afternoon."

Her friend closed the compact and looked hard at Mary. "*All* with your gang."

"Sure. Doesn't it sound like fun?"

Kelly dropped the compact back into her tiny purse and looked down at her hands. "I thought we'd be able to spend some time together alone while I was here."

"But we'll have lots of time alone," Mary said as the car sputtered to a stop outside the Bubnik's apartment building. "Really."

Kelly Kay didn't seem convinced. Her face had tightened into a pout. For the first time since her arrival, Mary had a sinking feeling that perhaps their reunion wasn't going to go as smoothly as she'd imagined. But she quickly brushed it off.

"We're going to have a wonderful holiday together," Mary told herself confidently as she hurried to get Kelly's luggage out of the boot. "I just know it."

Chapter Five

Tuesday was D-Day for Rocky – the Dreaded Dress Day. And it was as awful as she had imagined it would be. Rocky stood in the girl's department of the Base Exchange, holding a pink lace dress at arm's length. She hoped desperately that no one from her school would see her.

"I don't like it," Rocky announced, wrinkling her nose.

Mrs Garcia folded her arms sternly across her chest. "What don't you like about it?"

Rocky shrugged. "Everything."

"You said that about every dress on the rack," her mother said, clenching her teeth. She was obviously running out of patience. "Now I like this one, and I want you to at least try it on."

"But what if I hate it?" Rocky asked defiantly.

Mrs Garcia threw her hands in the air. "Then we won't buy it."

"Good."

Rocky marched into the dressing room stall, determined to hate the dress. She wanted to get this over with as quickly as possible, so she only took off her trousers and sweatshirt and left on her black-and-white socks and red hi-top baseball boots. She threw her clothes in a pile on the floor and dropped the frothy pink dress over her head.

"I'm sure I look like a total wimp," Rocky mumbled to herself. She could already hear her brothers hooting with laughter at the sight of her in the dress.

"Rochelle, are you dressed yet?" her mother called from outside.

"No," Rocky replied. She wasn't eager to step out and show anyone else what she looked like.

The saleslady wrenched open the door without knocking. "Let me see how it looks, dear," she said, giving Rocky the once-over.

Rocky glowered at her. Why did sales ladies always have to do that? A person could be standing there in her underwear, and they wouldn't care if the entire shop saw.

"Close the door!" Rocky barked, trying to flatten herself against the wall of the tiny room.

The saleslady ignored her and opened the door even wider. "You look lovely. Now come and show your mother."

Rocky peered out of the door to make sure no one was looking. Then, keeping close to the racks, she inched her way toward her mother.

"Doesn't she look nice?" the woman said to Mrs Garcia. "It's a perfect fit."

"It looks wonderful," Mrs Garcia replied, giving Rocky her smile of approval. Rocky could tell it was going to be a bit harder to convince her mom that she hated it.

"Why don't you come over here, and look in this big mirror," the sales lady suggested, "while I take your mother to the shoe department? I've just the right sandals to match that dress."

The two women hurried off down the aisle as Rocky stepped in front of the three-way mirror. She stared intently at her reflection. A dark-haired girl in a pink cloud of a dress looked back at her. She had to admit, the outfit didn't look all that bad. In fact, she thought with a small smile, she looked pretty good. Rocky did a pirouette and watched her skirt billow out around her.

As she turned, Rocky caught sight of a familiar face reflected in the mirror. She froze in mid-spin.

There, standing less than ten feet from her, was Russell Stokes, the coolest boy in the sixth grade. To make matters worse, two of his best friends were standing behind him — Todd Bramly and Josh Taylor.

"Hey, Garcia, is that really you?" Russell asked, a slow grin spreading across his face.

Rocky put her hands on her hips and tilted her chin up. "Yeah, it's me," she shot back. "The one and only. What're you doing in the girls department?" she challenged.

Russell nudged his friend Todd with his elbow and chuckled. "Just checking out the merchandise."

"Oh, I thought you were looking for an Easter bonnet," Rocky retorted.

Russell threw back his head and laughed. "That's a good one!" Then he suddenly asked, "Hey, are you going to the big Easter egg hunt?"

"Sure. I've already got my team together," Rocky replied proudly, feeling a bit more comfortable. Even though she was wearing a dress, this seemed to be a normal conversation. "How about you?"

"Yep. I wouldn't miss it for the world," he said, brushing a lock of his dark hair off his forehead. "Should be a great day."

"My friends and I can't wait," Rocky added, feeling better with each passing second. This was about to go on record as the longest conversation she had ever had with Russell. "We'll probably get our pictures in the paper when we win."

"When you win?" The tall boy grinned confidently. "I hate to break it to you, but we've got the first place all wrapped up."

"Oh, yeah?" Rocky put one hand on her hip. "What makes you so sure?"

"Because six guys can beat six girls any old day."

That did it. Her brothers were always telling her boys were better than girls, and Rocky'd had enough.

"Listen, you jerk," she snapped, "I could beat you *and* your friends with both hands tied behind my back."

Todd nudged Russell from behind. "Did you hear what she called you?"

"Yeah." Russell turned coolly to his friends. "But I think Miss Garcia is a little confused. Obviously she hasn't looked in a mirror lately."

Rocky narrowed her eyes. "What's that supposed to mean?"

Russell cocked his head to one side. "Are you wearing that dress to the egg hunt, by any chance?"

She rolled her eyes at the ceiling. "Of course I am. That's what Easter dresses are for."

Suddenly Russell burst out laughing. He ribbed his friends and they joined in.

Rocky's hands tightened into fists as she watched

them. "It's not that funny, you jerks. You're acting as if you've never seen a girl in a dress before."

"Not one that looked like that!" Josh Taylor exclaimed, pointing at Rocky.

"You wear that to the Easter egg hunt," Russell added, "and you'll be laughed out of the park."

Rocky was boiling inside. The one thing she hated most was being laughed at. She was standing beside a display of pastel-coloured Easter bunnies and chicks mounted on top of one of the clothing racks. Without thinking she swept the whole display into her arms and started throwing it at the boys.

"Hey, wait! Stop!" they cried, spluttering with laughter. Todd tripped over Josh attempting to get away from her and tumbled onto the floor.

Russell ducked behind a mannequin, but Rocky kept a stream of fuzzy missiles aimed at his head.

"What's going on here?" the saleslady shouted as she ran through the dress racks, clutching two shoe boxes to her chest. "You stop that this instant, do you hear?"

Rocky heard, but she wasn't going to stop. When she had thrown everything on the Easter display, she started on the hats and scarves nearby.

Meanwhile, Russell retreated toward the front door, still holding the mannequin in front of him for protection.

46

"Chicken!" Rocky yelled. "What are you, scared of a girl?"

Russell dumped the mannequin on its side by the door and the three boys fled outside.

"Rocky!" Mrs Garcia grabbed her daughter by the shoulders. "What's the matter with you?"

"There's nothing the matter with me," Rocky shouted. "It's this stupid dress!" She fought hard to keep her tears back. "Everyone's laughing at me."

Mrs Garcia spoke in a low voice, trying to get Rocky to calm down. "They're not laughing at your dress, Rocky. They're laughing at what you're wearing *with* it." She spun Rocky round to face the mirror and pointed at her feet. Rocky gasped at what she saw.

From her head to her knees was a pretty girl in a pink dress. But from her knees down she looked like a clown. An old band-aid dangled from one scraped knee. Her black-and-white striped socks made her calves look like barber poles. And her red hi-top baseball boots made her feet look huge.

"I *do* look like a jerk," she murmured to herself. "Russell must think I'm a complete, total idiot."

By this time a small crowd had gathered at the edge of the girls department. Rocky could hear them chuckling behind her and turned. To her horror she recognized five more classmates from school – all pointing and laughing at her.

47

Rocky wanted to sink right into the floor. All of her worst fears had come true. She was being humiliated in front of the entire air force base.

"Why don't you take a picture!" Rocky shrieked at the crowd. "It'll last longer."

Then she spun on her heel and stumbled toward the dressing room. As Rocky passed her mother, she rasped, "I am never wearing another dress as long as I live!"

Chapter Six

"I've got the rules for the Easter egg hunt," McGee announced to Gwen and Zan. They'd arrived early for their ballet class and stood slumped against the ballet *barre*. McGee waved the entry form at her friends. "Here are the prizes. The winning team will receive gift certificates to the Toy Gallery and tickets to a Cincinnati Reds game." McGee grinned at her friends. "Isn't that great?"

Gwen yawned. "It's great if you like to watch a bunch of guys running around getting sweaty."

"*And*," McGee continued, "free passes to WonderWorld amusement park."

"That's kids stuff," called Courtney Clay, who was in the middle of the splits on the opposite side of the room. She touched her head to her knee. "Page, Alice, and I are much more interested in the cash prize."

"Cash prize?" McGee blinked at her.

"Yes. Read on," Courtney said airily. "You haven't got to the good part."

McGee scanned the entry carefully. "One thousand dollars will be donated to the winner's charity of choice."

"Of course, we'll give our prize money to the ballet Academy," Courtney declared, lifting her head to smile sickeningly at the girls.

"That's if you win," Gwen said, returning her smile. "Which you won't."

Before Courtney could reply, the studio door flew open and banged against the wall. Rocky stomped into the room and marched straight over to the gang. She slammed her backpack down on the floor and barked, "Don't ask!"

McGee looked at Gwen and Zan, then back at Rocky. "Don't ask what?"

"Don't ask me about Easter dresses, or Russell Stokes, or the entire nosy sixth grade from Curtis-Dobbs Elementary."

"I guess your mom took you shopping," Zan said softly.

"Yeah." Rocky delivered a vicious karate kick into the air. "For the last time."

"That bad, huh?" Gwen pushed her glasses up onto her nose.

Rocky answered her with a scowl.

"Here." Gwen pushed the entry form in front of Rocky's nose. "Maybe that'll make you feel better. Look at the prizes we're going to win."

Rocky turned her head away. "Nothing could make me feel better, except – "

"Beating the Bunheads?" McGee whispered, leaning forward conspiratorially.

"What about the Bunheads?" Rocky shot a dirty look across the room at Courtney and her friends.

"They've entered the Easter egg hunt," Zan explained, "and they're convinced they're going to win."

"Over my dead body," Rocky declared fiercely. "We'll pulverize them. We'll leave them in the dust." She slammed her fist into her palm. "We'll send them a postcard from WonderWorld."

"That's the spirit!" McGee exclaimed, clapping her on the back.

"Ta-da!" Mary Bubnik shouted from the studio door. Her grin stretched from ear to ear. With a sweeping gesture she announced, "And now, presenting my very best friend in the whole wide world – Miss Kelly Kay Kingston!"

The entire class stared at the door but no one

came through it. Mary looked back at the gang and whispered loudly, "She's shy."

"Embarrassed, is more like it," Gwen murmured under her breath.

"I'll go and get her." Mary Bubnik skipped out of the studio and they heard another voice just outside the door rasp, "Mary, how could you?"

"See?" Gwen said, executing a side stretch. "I told you."

Zan nodded. "Sometimes Mary gets a little carried away."

At that moment, Annie Springer, their teacher, stepped into the room. She was followed by Mary Bubnik and a tall, red-haired girl dressed in a shiny pink leotard, with matching head band and leg warmers.

"That's Kelly Kay?" McGee gasped. "I don't believe it."

"Yeah, look at her hair," Gwen whispered out the corner of her mouth.

Kelly Kay had pulled her hair into a tiny knot on the top of her head.

"That bun is so tight," Rocky hissed, "I'm surprised her eyes don't pop out of her head."

"I hate to say this," McGee said quietly, "but she looks more like a Bunhead than the Bunheads."

"Maybe that's just the style back in Oklahoma," Zan suggested, trying to be nice.

"Maybe," Rocky replied. They watched Kelly walk across the floor with her feet in the same exaggerated turn-out as the Bunheads. "But I doubt it."

Annie Springer clapped her hands to get everyone's attention. "Class, Mary Bubnik has brought a guest today." She drew Mary Bubnik and her friend to the front of the room. "This is Kelly Kay Kingston, and she's visiting Mary from Oklahoma City."

"Hi, Kelly Kay," the class greeted her, almost in unison, which made everyone laugh.

'Did you know that one of America's most famous ballerinas was from Oklahoma?" Annie informed the class.

"Really?" Mary Bubnik exclaimed. "Who?"

"Maria Tallchief," Courtney and Kelly Kay replied at the same time.

The two girls looked at each other and smiled.

"I'm from Oklahoma," Mary Bubnik said, shaking her head. "I wonder why I didn't know that."

"Every real ballerina knows that," Courtney said smugly. "Maria Tallchief danced for the N.Y.C.B."

"What's that?" Mary Bubnik asked.

Courtney looked down her nose at Mary. "The New York City Ballet."

"Only the most famous dance company in America," Kelly explained.

"Maria Tallchief was one of their finest ballerinas," Courtney added, smiling at Kelly Kay.

Rocky nudged McGee. "Uh-oh. Courtney and Kelly seem to be getting along well."

"Maybe she's just trying to be friendly," Zan said generously.

"All right, girls, time to begin our warm-ups," Annie Springer announced. "Take your places at the *barre*."

Kelly Kay stood between Mary and the rest of the gang. "Why don't we warm up with those girls over there?" she whispered.

"Because they're not my friends," Mary Bubnik said as the music for *pliés* began.

"They're not?" Kelly look surprised. "But they look like serious dancers."

"Yeah," Gwen called over Mary's shoulders. "Seriously deranged."

Mary Bubnik giggled and then gestured with her thumb toward the gang. "*These* are my friends."

Rocky, whose wild mane of hair exploded out from her head, clutched the *barre* at the front of the line. Behind her, wearing a black leotard that had faded to a funny green and pink tights with several ladders in the legs, stood McGee. Zan, with her tall-girl slump, and Gwen, with her bulging waistline, completed the rag-tag crew.

Disappointment showed plainly all over Kelly Kay's face as she turned to face the girls. "Oh. What a surprise."

Mary rattled off everyone's names but Kelly Kay

didn't seem to notice. She was too busy concentrating on her *port de bras*, making sure her arm movements were fluid and graceful. Mary beamed at the gang and said, "She's good, isn't she?"

"Yeah," Rocky replied. Then she added under her breath, "Almost too good."

After the class had finished their warm-ups at the *barre*, Annie Springer instructed them to step into the center of the studio to begin their floor exercise.

As they stepped forward, Kelly looked critically at McGee. "They let you come to dance class with all those holes in your leotard?"

"But of course," McGee quipped. "This is the new look. Didn't you know that?"

"Sort of Punk Ballerina," Gwen added with a chuckle.

Kelly Kay ignored her joke and pointed at McGee's leg. "There's a ladder in your tights, too. Did you know that?"

All five girls stared at Kelly Kay in amazement. Rocky put her hands on her hips. "What is this, a fashion show?"

"No." Kelly Kay blushed. "It's just that, back in Oklahoma, they'd never let you into class dressed like that."

"Well . . ." McGee shrugged light-heartedly, "it's a good thing I'm not in Oklahoma."

Miss Springer asked each girl to do a series of

turns *en pointe*. One by one, the girls spun across the room. Finally it was Kelly's turn, and she performed her *pique* turns with perfect grace.

"Very nice, Kelly," Annie Springer said with an approving smile. "Now it's your turn, Mary."

Mary Bubnik eagerly tried to copy Kelly Kay's movements, extending her leg, then lifting her other toe to her knee, and turning. But halfway across the floor she got dizzy and stumbled over her feet, nearly falling to the floor.

Courtney and the Bunheads burst into the giggles.

"Take it more slowly next time," Miss Springer advised with an encouraging smile.

"And don't forget to spot," Courtney added smugly.

"What's that?" Mary asked innocently.

"It's focusing your eyes on one place when you turn," Kelly explained. She shook her head in amazement. "I can't believe you didn't know that."

Mary felt her face growing hot with embarrassment. "I'm sure I knew it," she said quickly. "I guess I just forgot."

"Yeah, sure," Page Tuttle said, rolling her eyes.

Rocky, who was still in a grumpy mood, sprang forward with her fists clenched. "Listen, Page, you better watch your mouth, or you'll *see* spots."

Page stuck out her tongue but kept quiet.

"Now, class," Annie announced, "pair up for *grand jetés*."

Before Mary knew what had happened, Kelly Kay had taken a place in line next to Courtney Clay, the leader of the Bunheads.

"I don't believe it!" McGee gasped.

"She doesn't mean anything by it," Zan whispered, squeezing Mary's limp hand.

"Oh, I know," Mary replied lightly. "Kelly Kay's just trying to be friendly." Mary Bubnik mustered a game smile, but there was no joy in her voice.

The music began and Kelly and Courtney leaped across the studio floor. As she passed, Kelly Kay smiled at Mary but it was one of those "I'm-better-than-you" smiles that Mary had never seen on her friend's face before. Mary felt as if she'd been punched in the stomach.

"She's really pretty good." McGee patted Mary Bubnik on the shoulder.

"She's only been here twenty minutes," Zan added brightly, "and she fits right in."

No one was saying exactly what they were thinking because they didn't want to hurt Mary's feelings.

"She and Courtney act as if they've known each other for years." Gwen plastered a cheerful grin on her face. "Isn't that amazing?"

"Amazing," Mary replied quietly.

Her friends exchanged worried looks. Mary Bubnik didn't sound her usual self at all.

After class Kelly Kay skipped to Mary and said, "This was so much fun! I'm glad you brought me along."

Mary was pleased to see her friend so happy. She just wished Kelly had spent more time with her during the lesson.

When the girls trooped into the dressing room, Gwen called out, "How about going over to Hi's for something to eat?"

"Sounds good to me," McGee said.

"Me, too," Mary Bubnik cried. She knew it would be a perfect opportunity for Kelly Kay and her friends to get better acquainted.

"Will the other girls be going there?" Kelly asked, her eyes shining with enthusiasm.

"What other girls?" Mary Bubnik replied.

"Courtney and Page," Kelly said as she changed into her plaid jumper and white lace blouse.

"No." Mary looked perplexed, then explained, "They never go there."

"Oh," Kelly said flatly. "What kind of food does this restaurant serve?"

"Oh, all kinds of great stuff," Gwen gushed. "Pizza, egg rolls, and milk shakes with hidden surprises, like peanut butter — "

"Sounds great," Kelly interrupted, "but I'm watching my weight. We ballerinas have to stay skinny."

Gwen peered down self-consciously at her bulging midriff. "Yes, I suppose we ballerinas do."

"You see, back in Oklahoma," Kelly continued, checking her reflection in the mirror, "we had a special diet for dancing."

"Well, so do we," McGee piped up. "But this is the spring holiday." She grinned broadly. "And we have a special diet for *that*!"

"While we're at Hi's," Zan added, "we can go over our plans for our march to save the Academy."

"It's too bad about your school," Kelly Kay said. "Back in Oklahoma our ballet school would never have any money problems."

"Of course they wouldn't have the same problems!" Mary Bubnik said with a giggle. "The school is in Miss Lynn's basement."

"That's beside the point, Mary," Kelly snapped. "You know that dancers come from all over the city to have lessons there. In fact, we had eighty kids trying out for our production of *The Nutcracker*."

"What a coincidence!" Mary Bubnik's face suddenly lit up. "That's how we all met, doing *The Nutcracker*. We played the mice."

"The mice are the most insignificant characters in the play," Kelly Kay sniffed.

"Not the way we played them," McGee cracked.

"Our mice were spectacular," Zan said proudly. "Everyone said so."

"That's nice," Kelly said, picking a piece of lint off of her dress. "Back in Oklahoma, some important dance critics wrote that our Nutcracker was the very best they'd ever seen."

"Oh, really?" Rocky raised an eyebrow. "That's great, Kelly. Isn't that great, everyone?"

Zan, Gwen, and McGee nodded dutifully. "Great."

"So are we going to Hi's, or not?" Gwen asked.

Kelly Kay turned to Mary and said, "I'm kind of tired. That class was a real workout."

"Gee, I really wanted you to meet Hi Lo," Mary said.

"I'd love to," Kelly Kay said, making a show of massaging a sore calf muscle. "But maybe another time, OK?"

"Well . . ." Mary tried to mask her disappointment with a smile. "If you really feel that way." She turned to face her pals. "I'll see y'all tomorrow at Zan's."

After the two girls had left the dressing room, Zan turned to the others and whispered urgently, "We've got a truly big problem."

"Bigger than winning the Easter egg hunt," Rocky said.

"Or saving the Academy," Gwen added.

"Yeah." McGee flipped up the brim of her baseball cap. "How are we going to break it to Mary that her best friend in the whole world is a . . . *Bunhead.*"

60

Chapter Seven

The next day, Baumgartner's department store was packed with people doing their last minute shopping for Easter. A line of girls and their mothers stretched the length of the pre-teen department out into the hall by the elevators. They were all waiting to get into the four dressing rooms.

The store was terribly hot and stuffy and Rocky was starting to sweat. She glanced sideways at the only man in the girls' department — her father.

Sergeant Garcia stood stiffly in his crisp blue military uniform beside a rack of spring dresses. He did not look happy. He had marched Rocky into the department store, grabbed three dresses off the rack at random, and handed them to the saleslady with the instructions: "Whichever one fits her, that's the one we'll take."

Rocky couldn't believe it. Her dad hadn't even asked for her opinion. Worst of all, he'd grabbed three of the most hideous dresses she'd ever seen in her life.

"Why didn't I take the pink dress Mom picked out for me?" Rocky moaned to herself. She checked her watch. Not only was she about to buy an ugly dress but she was already half an hour late to Zan's for the meeting. Luckily the Reeds only lived a few blocks from the centre of town and Rocky knew she could get there in five minutes. If she ever got out of Baumgartner's.

Rocky glanced at her watch again. Then a light bulb went on in her head. She decided she could get out of trying on those dresses – but she needed some help.

"Psst! Dad?" Rocky whispered from her place in line.

Sergeant Garcia gave her an irritated look. "What is it?"

"I have got to go to the ladies."

His eyes widened. "Now?"

"Yes." Rocky contorted her face into a desperate look. "Now!"

"I see." The sergeant cleared his throat uneasily. "Do you need me to, um . . . go with you?"

"No, Dad!" Rocky blurted quickly. "Just hold my place and I'll be right back."

Her father hesitated for a moment, then nodded his head. "OK. But make it snappy." He set a timer on his digital watch. "You've got five minutes. If you're not back by then, I'm buying you a dress whether it fits or not."

"Yes, sir."

"And you'll *have* to wear it."

"I understand, sir," Rocky replied, backing away down the aisle toward the ladies lounge. As soon as she turned the corner, Rocky ran for all she was worth. "Please, *please* let me have a quarter," she whispered as she ran.

Gwen and McGee were the first to arrive at Zan's house for the meeting. They'd each brought some food for the gang to munch on.

"This is brain food to help us think better," McGee announced, holding up a tray of celery and carrot sticks covered in plastic wrap. She set the tray on the butcher block table in Zan's kitchen.

"And this" — Gwen held up a bright plastic sack marked "Gourmet Jelly Beans' and a box of chocolate bunnies — "this is to make it fun to think!"

"How wonderful!" Zan arranged the treats in a pretty pattern on a big silver platter. "My mom always says that the secret to throwing a successful party is having good food or great activities."

"And we have both," McGee declared.

Zan led the girls into the sitting room, where she'd arranged sheets of poster board, felt pens and construction paper in neat rows along the coffee table.

"Where's Mary Bubnik?" McGee asked. "And Kelly Kay?"

"With any luck," Gwen murmured in an exaggerated southern accent, "Kelly went back to Oh-kla-ho-ma."

Zan started to laugh, then covered her mouth. "We shouldn't make fun of her," she scolded gently. "After all, she is Mary's friend. There must be something to like about her."

"I think she's a snob," Gwen declared, popping several jellybeans into her mouth.

"And a show-off." McGee bit off a piece of carrot with a loud crunch for emphasis.

"Well, it's hard to be new," Zan said. "Maybe Kelly Kay was just trying to impress us."

"Impress the Bunheads, is more like it." Gwen flopped down on one of the thick cushions Zan had placed round the coffee table. "I think she hardly noticed us at all."

"Maybe we should give her another chance,"

McGee said. "For Mary's sake." She grinned mischievously at her friends. "When Kelly gets here this afternoon, we'll kill her with kindness."

"That's going to be a little difficult," Zan said, "since she's not coming."

"What?" Gwen nearly choked on a chocolate rabbit ear. "How come?"

"Mary phoned just before you guys came and told me Kelly Kay wasn't feeling very well."

Gwen snorted. "A likely story. What about the march tomorrow? Is she going to make it?"

"Don't forget the Easter egg hunt," McGee added. "We won't have much of a team without them."

"Mary promised me they'd be there," Zan reassured them. She frowned and added, "she sounded sad."

"I don't blame her," Gwen said. "If I had a friend like Kelly Kay, I'd be *really* depressed."

The phone rang and Zan jumped up to answer it. "Maybe that's Mary, calling to say — "

"She's sent Kelly Kay back to Oh-kla-ho-ma!" Gwen and McGee chorused.

"You guys are awful!" Zan giggled as she picked up the receiver. "Hello?"

Static crackled on the line. Finally Zan heard a distant voice whisper. "It's me."

"Rocky? Why aren't you here?"

65

"I'm at Baumgartner's department store," came the hissed reply. "With my dad."

"Your father?" Zan frowned. "It sounds bad."

"It is. He says if I don't pick out a dress today, he's going to confine me to quarters for the rest of my life, and put me on permanent KP."

"Well, pick one out."

"But he's making me try on these awful little girly things," Rocky explained. "I really need your help."

"Where are you again?"

"In the ladies' cloakroom. There's a pay phone here."

Just then there was a loud click on the line and a recording announced, "Your three minutes are up. Please deposit fifteen cents immediately."

"I haven't got fifteen cents," Rocky snapped.

Zan heard a series of loud crunches that sounded like Rocky was punching the phone. Then Rocky's voice pleaded, "Come quick, please. I'll be in the dressing room of the girls wear department. And don't let my dad — "

Then there was silence. Zan hung up the phone and faced the gang. "We've got another crisis. Rocky's in trouble down at Baumgartner's, and she needs our help right now."

"But what about the posters?" Gwen asked. "And our snacks?"

"They'll have to wait." Zan was already at the front door. "Come on. I'll explain on the way."

"Oh, I hate to see good food go to waste." Gwen took the entire plate of jellybeans and chocolate bunnies and dumped it into her blue dance bag.

"Do you want the celery and carrot sticks?" Zan asked.

"You must be joking. That's rabbit food. Save it for the Easter Bunny."

By the time the girls reached Baumgartner's, ten minutes had passed. McGee led Zan and Gwen up the escalator to the girls department.

"There she is!" McGee ponted to the forlorn figure of a dark-haired girl being led into a dressing room by a saleslady.

"And there *he* is!" Gwen gestured to the uniformed man standing at attention by the three-way mirror, his hands clasped behind his back.

"Sergeant Garcia looks as if he's standing guard," Zan said.

"He is," McGee whispered back. She pulled the others into a tight huddle. "We have got to get into that dressing room without him seeing us."

"But there's a long queue," Gwen replied, nodding at the row of girls clutching dresses in their arms outside the entrance to the dressing room. "It'll take forever to get in."

"Wait a minute." McGee spotted a door marked "Employees Only" behind the cash register. A broad grin spread across her face. "I bet that will lead us to Rocky. Come on!"

The rack beside them was marked half-price. McGee grabbed a dress off it and the others followed suit. Holding the dresses in front of their faces, McGee led the girls straight for the employee's door. McGee threw it open, and nearly collided with a young salesgirl on the other side.

"What do you think you're doing?" the girl demanded.

McGee froze, unable to think of a quick reply. Then Gwen spoke up. "My father owns this store, and we're going to a dressing room. I'm Gwendolyn Baumgartner." She narrowed her eyes at the salesgirl. "Don't you recognize me?"

"I – I'm sorry, I don't," the salesgirl sputtered. "You see, I'm new here."

Gwen clucked disapprovingly. "I thought so." She motioned for Zan and McGee to go ahead of her through the door. Then she turned and sniffed, "Next time you'll know better."

They left the astounded salesgirl behind and ran round the corner. A row of four dressing rooms greeted them.

"How are we going to know which one Rocky's in?" Gwen wondered.

Behind the curtained cubicle nearest the gang a familiar voice complained loudly, "I hate this!"

"Rocky," Zan whispered. "We're here."

The curtain flew open and Rocky stuck her head out. "It's about time."

Her dark hair framed her face like an angry storm cloud. A straw hat with little flowers perched on top of her head. She was wearing a dress covered in little daisies with a white lace collar. On her feet she wore white lace anklets and black patent leather shoes.

"Oh, Rocky!" Zan gasped. "You look . . . well . . ."

"Terrible!" Gwen finished for her.

Rocky surprised them all by saying, "I know." Then her lower lip began to quiver. "Dad said if I didn't take the dress Mom picked, he'd choose one. And he did."

"Well, that would look awfully nice on a first-grader," Gwen cracked.

Rocky made a face. "Thanks a lot. But the other choices are even worse." She gestured to the lacy dresses that hung on the hook behind her.

"Maybe we could go and find you something better," Zan suggested.

"Great idea," Rocky said. "I knew I could count on you guys." She checked her watch. "But you better work fast, my dad is losing his patience."

"What do you like?" Gwen asked.

Rocky squinted one eye shut, trying to think. "Something that's not frilly and not pink or blue or yellow. Oh, and I hate anything that has flowers or lace on it."

"Hmmm." McGee scratched her chin. "That gives us a place to start. Here." She thrust the dress she'd been holding into Rocky's arms. "Hold this while we go and look."

"Hey!" Rocky's eyes lit up. "Where'd you get this?"

McGee shrugged. "Off the sales rack. I just grabbed the first thing I could find."

"Let me see." Rocky held the narrow dress up to her body. "It's a weird pattern – like a zebra stripe." The dress had a scoop neck, with long sleeves, and was made out of a shiny, stretchy material. "I think I like it."

"I don't know," Gwen said, shaking her head. "Black and white isn't very Easter-y."

"That's what makes it so cool." Rocky was already peeling off the lacy flowered dress her father had chosen.

"What are you doing?" Zan exclaimed.

"I'm going to try it on," Rocky replied. She stepped into the dress and pulled it up around her shoulders. It fitted like a glove.

"Wow." Gwen adjusted her glasses and stared at Rocky in amazement. "It makes you look *years* older."

"It truly does," Zan breathed. "Especially if you wear your hair up."

Rocky grabbed her thick dark mane and pulled it up on top of her head. "Like this?"

"Oh, yes!" Zan cried. "Now you look like a night club singer."

McGee shook her head grimly. "Your parents will never let you wear something like that."

"Rochelle!" a male voice boomed down the hall. "Your time is up, young lady. Whatever you've got on now — that's what we're buying."

A slow smile spread across Rocky's face. "Is that an order?"

"You'd better believe it!" Sergeant Garcia barked. "Now get out here, on the double."

"Yes, sir!"

With a thumbs-up to the gang, Rocky pulled back the curtain and sashayed out to meet her father.

Chapter Eight

On Saturday morning, Mary Bubnik and Kelly Kay sat in the car, waiting for Mrs Bubnik to drive them to the Fair. They were both wearing their Easter dresses, Mary in her bright blue one, and Kelly wearing a new lavender dress with a drop waist and sash at the hip. Each girl held an empty Easter basket in her lap. Mary and Kelly had twisted pink and yellow ribbons around the handles, then tied them up so that the ribbons would hang in long streamers.

Mary kept thinking that they should be having a good time. After all, she had looked forward to Kelly's arrival for ages, but things just weren't turning out the way she wanted at all.

"I'm glad we don't have to drive there with all your friends," Kelly Kay said, smoothing the sash on her dress.

"What's wrong with my friends?" Mary asked.

"Well, I really don't want to have to be the one to tell you," Kelly Kay replied, blinking her clear blue eyes.

"There isn't anything wrong with my friends," Mary insisted, "and that's why you can't tell me."

"Oh, I don't know about that." Kelly Kay tossed her hair over her shoulder with a flick of her hand. "Why does Zan slump all the time, and why does Rocky always try to start a fight with everybody?"

"Zan doesn't always slump, and Rocky doesn't start fights," Mary retorted. "She just doesn't like to see other people being picked on."

"And that other one — what's her name, Gwen?" Kelly Kay asked off-handedly. "She should really lose some weight."

"Gwen is one of the nicest and cleverest people I know," Mary shot back.

"Then there's McGee. Now what kind of a name is that for a girl?" Kelly scoffed.

"It's a great name for a girl, especially someone who is a real star." Mary felt close to tears.

"A star?" Kelly repeated.

"Yes. She's a star hockey player," Mary said angrily. "And even if she wasn't, she'd still be my friend."

"Sorry I said anything." Kelly Kay bit her lip and stared out the window at the bus that had pulled up to the curb near the apartment. "Do you think this car will make it to the park without falling apart? Maybe I should take the bus."

"It'll get us there, Kelly Kay, don't worry." Mary Bubnik took several deep breaths, trying not to lose her temper. Then she decided to change the subject. "Hey, Kelly Kay, remember how we used to hate ol' Marla Huddleston?"

"*Hate* her?" Kelly Kay stared at her like she was crazy. "Mary, that was ages ago. Marla and I are best friends now."

Mary's heart dropped like a stone. "I can't believe it! Marla is the worst stuck-up snob in Oklahoma City! Did she change or something?"

"No, Mary." Kelly Kay turned her gaze on Mary Bubnik. "You're the one who's changed. *You've* become a snob."

"I have not!" Mary Bubnik said, jumping up in her seat and bonking her head against the ceiling. She winced and rubbed the top of her head. "That's not true!"

"Yes it is," Kelly Kay said through clenched teeth. "You act like Oklahoma's just this hick state."

"Well, you act like it's the center of the universe," Mary retorted, feeling her face redden with anger.

"All you've ever talked about in your letters is your

74

stupid new friends and this dumb little town." Kelly Kay made a face and continued in a sing-song voice, "Deerfield this and Deerfield that."

"You don't know anything about Deerfield," Mary Bubnik cut in.

Kelly Kay crossed her arms. "And I don't want to."

"Well, it's just as good as Oklahoma," Mary persisted.

"You really have changed, Mary." Kelly Kay turned away and checked her reflection in the driving mirror. "You've become a completely different person."

"I was just thinking the same thing about you." Mary crossed her arms and glared at her friend. "Since when did you start looking at yourself in the mirror every two seconds?"

Kelly's eyes suddenly shone with tears. "You never used to say mean things like that, Mary. You were always sweet before." She pulled a tiny lace hankie with her initials monogrammed on it from her glove and dabbed at her eyes. "I think you've changed for the worse . . ."

At the moment Mrs Bubnik pulled open the car door and hopped in the driver's seat. "Sorry I'm late, girls. But it took me a little longer than usual to get myself ready."

Mary turned away from Kelly and stared out of the window.

As Mrs Bubnik backed the car out of the driveway, she asked cheerfully, "Are you two looking forward to the Spring Fest? This is quite an event."

"Uh-huh," Mary murmured.

"Where are you meeting your friends, Mary?" Mrs Bubnik asked.

"Near the entrance to the park," Mary Bubnik replied dully.

They rode in silence for a while.

Finally Mrs Bubnik said, "Well, Mr Toad is in fine spirits since he had his check-up." She patted the dashboard. "Aren't you, Mr Toad?"

There was no response from the backseat. At the trafficlights Mrs Bubnik turned round. "It's awfully quiet back there. Anything wrong?"

"No," Kelly Kay replied, staring at the ribbon on her Easter basket.

Mary attempted a smile so her mother wouldn't ask any more questions. She had never felt so depressed in her entire life. It was unbelievable that she and her best friend were having this fight. Back in Oklahoma, they never fought at all.

When Mrs Bubnik pulled the car into the parking area of the city park, the Spring Fest was in full swing. A big banner was draped across the entrance, with bunches of helium balloons tied at each end. Across the green, a brass band played "The Easter Parade" in the bandstand. All along the edge of the park, civic clubs, like the Kiwanis and the Elks Lodge, had set up gaily decorated booths selling hot dogs and ice cream.

Anxious to get out of the car and away from Kelly Kay, Mary Bubnik said, "Mom, drop us off here."

Mrs Bubnik put on the brakes and pulled to a stop. "Are you sure you girls are all right?"

"Positive." Mary hopped out of the car and added, "We'll be even better when we win the Easter egg hunt."

That seemed to reassure her mother. As she drove off, she called, "Good luck!" Then she beeped the horn merrily until she was round the corner.

"Does she have to do that?" Kelly asked. "It's embarrassing. Everyone is staring at us."

Normally Mary would have agreed with Kelly Kay, but today she just shrugged. "Let 'em."

Mary turned to walk down one of the aisles of booths. "Come on," Mary called to Kelly Kay. "Let's go and find the gang."

"I think I've found them." Kelly had stepped beside a booth selling painted eggs. Directly behind it was an open, grassy area where Zan and the others had gathered.

Zan carried a huge sign that proclaimed in bright green letters, "SAVE D.A.D." She was wearing a pale floral print dress that hung loosely on her slender frame. Gwen and McGee stood beside her, clutch-ing their own posters and banners. McGee wore a white skirt and blouse with a blue sailor collar. Gwen's Easter dress was mint green and covered in narrow silver stripes that her mother said made her look slimmer.

"Look!" Mary pointed at her friend. "McGee has brought a megaphone. She must have borrowed it from her hockey coach."

Kelly didn't respond. She was too busy gaping at the fourth member of the tiny group of protesters. "Look at Rocky," she gasped. "What on earth is she wearing?"

Rocky's dad, who never backs down on an order, had allowed her to buy the sleek black and white dress. But her mother had added certain conditions – she had to wear patent leather shoes and white anklets. And put a bow in her hair. Rocky had agreed, but she made sure the bow was a red one. That way it would match her red satin jacket, which she had draped over shoulders.

Mary couldn't answer Kelly's question. Even she had to admit that Rocky's outfit was unusual.

Just then McGee spotted Mary and she nudged the rest of the gang. They all hopped up and down, waving their posters and flyers at once. McGee put the megaphone to her mouth and shouted, "Mary Bubnik! Come on down!"

Mary burst out laughing. Then she shouted back, "We're coming!" She forgot for a second that she and Kelly Kay were mad at each other, and Mary took Kelly by the hand. "Come on!"

Kelly jerked her hand away and Mary stumbled forward, nearly crashing into a lemonade stand. "You go on without me," Kelly said.

"But why?"

"I don't want to demonstrate with you guys. It's not my ballet school." Kelly smoothed her dress carefully. "I'll see you later at the Easter egg hunt, OK?"

"Kelly Kay!" Mary Bubnik cried. "You said you were going to help. We need you."

"Sorry," was all Kelly said.

Mary watched her friend disappear into the crowd and, to her surprise, felt a huge wave of relief wash over her. She hated to admit it, but she was glad Kelly had gone.

Chapter Nine

"Heeeeere's Mary!" McGee announced through the megaphone as Mary Bubnik skipped up to meet the gang.

"Wow, everybody looks so pretty!" Mary exclaimed. "And Rocky, you just look fantastic in that dress."

"Thanks." Rocky beamed at McGee. "She picked it out for me."

"Where's Kelly Kay?" Gwen asked.

Mary Bubnik's face grew somber. "She decided she didn't want to do this. She'll meet us later at the Easter egg hunt." Mary noticed that her friends looked almost as relieved as she felt.

"OK, guys," McGee said, clapping her hands

together. "Let's get started. I think we should parade round the outside of the park and shout, 'Save D.A.D.'"

"And we should wave our signs like this." Rocky demonstrated by raising and lowering her sign rhythmically as she marched round them in a circle.

"Then we can hand out leaflets to anyone who has questions," Zan added.

McGee blew a shrill blast on the whistle round her neck and Rocky bellowed, "*Hut* – two, three, four; D.A.D. is what we're marching for!"

She led the girls in a military-style march round the concession stand. They passed people who smiled at them pleasantly and then continued on their way. But no one stopped to give them money, or even ask a question.

After they had circled the concession area twice, Rocky bellowed, "Marchers – *halt!*"

Zan immediately stopped and McGee, who was looking the other way, crashed right into her back.

"My leaflets!" Zan cried as little pieces of paper blew every which way. She bent forward to pick them up and Gwen tumbled over her back onto the ground. Mary Bubnik fell right on top of her.

"What are you trying to do, kill me?" Gwen shrieked from the bottom of the pile.

"I think your sign is caught in my hair," Mary Bubnik said, trying to untangle her curls.

"Well, your elbow is in my eye," Gwen complained.

"Someone is standing on my sign." McGee yanked on her poster with both hands and Rocky fell backward onto the ground with a loud, "Oomph!"

Meanwhile, Zan was crawling around on her hands and knees, picking up the scattered leaflets.

A few concerned people stopped to ask if they were all right, and that's when Rocky snapped her fingers. "I've got it!"

"Got what?" the girls asked as they struggled to stand up.

"This marching around and shouting is getting us nowhere," Rocky declared. "We need to be more upset." She gestured for the group to come close and they gathered round her in a huddle, their placards slung over their shoulders. "We're really upset that they're closing down the Academy, aren't we?"

"Of course!" they chorused.

"Then we have to *look* like it. We need to convince everybody here that we're sad and . . ." she lowered her voice meaningfully – "desperate."

"But how do we do that?" Mary Bubnik asked.

"Acting." Rocky had been to several drama classes on base and was the group's authority on the theatre. "My teacher told us that when we want to look sad, we have to think sad thoughts."

Mary Bubnik didn't have to think very hard to be sad. All she had to do was remember how it felt to be in the car with ex-best friend, Kelly Kay. She remembered how Kelly Kay had said she had changed for the worse. And how Kelly Kay had told her she was such a snob.

"Wow, Mary," Gwen said, noticing the grief-stricken look on Mary's face. "That's really good!"

"Very convincing," Rocky declared, patting her lightly on the shoulder.

Real tears filled Mary's eyes, and she wiped them away with her sleeve. "Thanks, you guys," she said huskily.

They practiced their tragic looks for a few minutes until Rocky was satisfied everyone looked miserable enough. "OK gang," she said finally, "let's do our stuff!"

Zan, still keeping her sad look on her face, pointed toward the park entrance. "I think we should take up a position right there, so everyone who comes here today can see us."

The girls trudged mournfully to the entrance, stopping every few feet to wail, "Save D.A.D.!" As they approached the grassy spot under the banner Gwen noticed a man in a blue blazer clutching a microphone.

83

Gwen jabbed McGee in the ribs. "That's Bob Beasely from Channel 29!"

They stared at the local reporter in awe as he interviewed someone in the crowd. His cameraman stood nearby, a large video camera slung over his shoulder.

"And he's got a television camera with him!" Mary Bubnik squealed.

"Camera!" Rocky immediately yanked the red bow her mother had made her wear out of her hair. Then she turned to the others and declared, "This is our big chance!"

McGee nodded excitedly. "Everybody, give it all you've got with the sad stuff – "

"*Now!*" Rocky barked.

McGee, Gwen, Zan, and Rocky suddenly cried, "Save D.A.D.! Please!"

Mary Bubnik thought of Kelly Kay somewhere out in that crowd, and how they might not be friends anymore after today, and fresh tears came to her eyes. "Please save D.A.D.!" Her voice rose to a high-pitched wail.

The TV reporter motioned to the cameraman to focus his lens on the five distraught girls. "What's going on here?" he asked, thrusting a microphone in McGee's face.

"If D.A.D. isn't saved, we'll never see each other

again!" Rocky cried, forcing out some anguished sobs.

Zan nodded and held her hand over her heart to show it was breaking.

Gwen pressed up next to McGee and leaned into the microphone. "We'll be split up," she shrieked.

"And sent all over the city," Zan moaned.

Mary Bubnik's tears suddenly streamed down her face. "We'll never be able to take ballet lessons together, and it'll be the worst thing that ever happened to us!"

The camera zoomed in for a close-up as she sobbed hysterically. A kind bystander handed her a tissue. "Thank you," she mumbled, blowing her nose.

"I'm a little confused," the reporter said. "What's wrong and what exactly do you need?" A crowd had begun to cluster around the girls, murmuring with curiosity.

"Money," Rocky wailed. "Lots of it."

"It's the only way D.A.D. can be saved," Gwen added, pushing her glasses up on the bridge of her nose.

"You *must* understand," Zan said, looking directly into the camera lens, "this is truly a tragedy."

"Hold it!" the cameraman shouted suddenly. He looked at the reporter and said, "Sorry, Bob, but I'm out of tape. I'll have to get some out of the van."

"You can't be serious?" Bob Beasely asked impatiently. He turned to the girls. "Don't go anywhere, we'll be right back." Then he followed the cameraman toward a white van parked by the curb. "I can't believe you! This is the first *We Care* story that we've had for ages, and you run out of tape!"

"Did you hear that?" Gwen crowed. "We've been chosen for Channel 29's *We Care* programme!"

"Wow!" Rocky whistled through her teeth. "We're going to be on television."

"And with Bob Beasely," Zan breathed happily.

"Yeah, people all over Ohio will see us and send money to the Academy," McGee said. "We'll be heroes."

"Boy, will Kelly Kay be sorry she missed this," Mary Bubnik said, shaking her head.

Rocky started giggling. "I wish I could see the Bunheads' faces when they watch the news. They'll be green with envy."

The bright signs fluttered in the breeze and passers by squinted to read the messages. Zan and Mary started handing out leaflets while they waited for the TV crew to come back.

"Attention, everyone!" a loudspeaker suddenly boomed across the park.

Rocky, Zan, Mary Bubnik, Gwen, and McGee froze in their tracks.

"The event you've all been waiting for – The

Annual Easter Egg Hunt — will be getting under way at the bandstand in exactly five minutes. All entrants will please take their places."

"Five minutes!" Mary Bubnik gasped. "The bandstand is the other side of the park." She hurriedly gathered up her sign and leaflets. "We've got to hurry."

"Wait a minute!" Gwen shouted. "What about our reporter?"

The girls hesitated, unsure of what to do.

"Look, we'll leave our signs here," McGee declared. "That way, he'll know we didn't run away. Then we'll catch up with him after the hunt."

"Super!" Rocky said as they hurried toward the starting line. "Now Bob Beasely can film us not only saving the Academy, but winning first prize at the Easter egg hunt."

Chapter Ten

"Wait! We can't start yet!" Mary Bubnik cried as the girls lined up at the starting line. Other teams were taking their places all along the thin plastic strip that stretched across the grass. "Kelly Kay's not here!"

"Well, they're not going to delay the Easter egg hunt just for Kelly," Gwen mumbled as she looped her basket over her arm.

Rocky crouched into a runner's position, her basket beside her. "We'll just have to go without her."

"Yeah," McGee said, assuming the same position as Rocky. "Our team will have to work harder 'cause we're one member short, but I think we can do it."

Mary stood on tiptoe, shading her eyes from the

sun. "I can't believe she's not here. Something must have happened."

"OK, kids," the starter's voice boomed over the loudspeaker. "Get ready to begin – and may the best team win!"

"Mary!" Gwen shouted. "Get in position!"

Mary Bubnik chewed one fingernail nervously. "I can't," she groaned. "I've got to find Kelly Kay. Y'all are going to have to go without me."

"Terrific!" McGee stood up and put her hands on her hips. "Now we're down to four members. They better start this thing before our team completely disappears – "

Her last word was covered by the blast of the starter's pistol. Suddenly hundreds of kids raced forward into the park, leaving the gang back at the starting line.

And there, leading the entire pack, were six girls in pink sweatshirts that had ballet dancers stenciled on the back.

·"Look at that!" Rocky gasped. "It's the Bunheads."

"And they're winning," McGee added in dismay.

"What are we waiting for?" Gwen shouted as she hoisted her basket up to her shoulder. "Come on!"

With one final glance at Mary Bubnik, the girls surged forward.

"Follow me!" Rocky shouted as she led the group

in a snake-like pattern through the hordes of Easter egg hunters.

"There's one!" McGee spotted a pale blue egg lying nestled between two boulders. She made a dive for it but three other kids got there before her.

Gwen spied a little grass nest cradling several eggs covered in gleaming tinfoil. It was perched on top of a prickly green bush. She shoved her glasses up on her nose and cried, "Chocolate!" Just as she reached for the nest, a small boy snatched it right out from under her nose and ran off across the green.

"Stop, thief!" Gwen roared in outrage.

"You've gotta be quick," another boy chuckled as he raced past her, a half-filled basket under his arm.

"And vicious," Gwen snarled. She turned to the gang and complained, "those chocolate eggs had my name all over them, and that little pipsqueak stole them."

"Forget about that," McGee called over her shoulder. "And keep looking."

Gwen hurried to keep up with Rocky and McGee. Zan soon joined them, declaring, "Our problem is, we don't have a plan."

"Isn't it a little late for that?" Gwen huffed. She was already out of breath from running.

Zan waved a piece of paper that she had tucked

into her basket. "This morning I made a list of likely places to look, and I think we should start with the trees. I bet no one is looking there."

McGee, who was busily examining a cluster of rocks, said, "Those are the first to go. I think we should keep close to the ground, and look under rocks and clumps of grass."

"I still think we should look in trees," Zan insisted. She pointed toward a small grove of oak trees that stood at the edge of the grassy knoll.

"Well, we better look somewhere," Gwen declared. "'Cause this hunt is half over, and we haven't found a single Easter egg." She turned her basket upside down to make her point.

Rocky veered to the right, leading the girls toward the tall oaks. The others fell in line behind her. Suddenly she stopped in her tracks, causing a few egg hunters to crash into her.

"For crying out loud!" a freckle-faced boy yelled. "Watch where you're going."

"Hey, cool it!" Rocky brandished her basket in his direction, "or you'll be wearing this for a hat."

"Why are we stopping?" Gwen called from the back of the line.

Rocky nodded in the direction she wanted them to look. "Russell Stokes and his team are right over there. I want to let them get ahead of us."

"So he can win?" Gwen shouted. "That's the dumbest thing I've ever heard!"

Rocky ducked behind her friends and murmured, "I don't want him to see me in a dress. He'll laugh at me, just like he did at the B.X."

"Geez Louise!" McGee cried, "I can't believe you'd let a jerky boy make us lose the egg hunt."

"We're not going to lose it," Rocky snapped, still keeping her back turned to Russell.

"That's right." McGee suddenly grabbed Rocky by the arm and dragged her up the steep hill in front of them. "We'll pass him, and he'll never know you were here."

"Yo, Rocky!" a voice shouted as the girls tried to clamber up the steep incline.

Rocky locked her knees and spun to face her pursuer. "What!" she challenged. She dropped her basket to the ground and tossed off her jacket.

"Oh, boy, here it comes," Gwen mumbled. "The Easter Day Massacre."

Russell who had just found a large silver egg, dropped it in his basket, and called, "Nice dress."

"Oh, yeah?" Rocky's eyes narrowed and she took several menacing steps toward him.

Russell raised one hand in self-defense. "No, I'm serious. It makes you look a lot older." He grinned and added, "You look cool."

"Do you really think so?"

The girls watched in amazement as a bright pink colour rushed to Rocky's cheeks. They'd never seen their friend blush before. She shook her thick mane of hair back over her shoulder and moved closer to Russell.

"This is just great!" Gwen wailed. "Now we've lost Rocky."

"Not to mention the rest of the Easter egg hunters." Zan made a sweeping motion over the field with her arm. There wasn't another team in sight.

"They must have all gone over the top of that hill." McGee hitched her basket up on her arm. "If we hurry, we can catch up with them."

The three girls struggled to run the rest of the way up the hill. When they reached the top, they looked down and saw the rest of the egg hunters far off in the distance.

Gwen dropped to her knees and gasped, "We'll never catch up. Not in a million years!"

After Mary Bubnik left her friends, she ran as hard as she could all over the park, searching for Kelly Kay. She checked every single booth and all of the concession stands. She even went back to the starting line of the Easter egg hunt, to see if maybe Kelly Kay had decided to enter late.

She slumped against the bandstand and murmured to herself, "Now where would I go if I were Kelly Kay, and I were upset?" Her eyes lit up. "I'd probably go to the ladies' cloakroom and lock myself in."

Mary headed for the cloakrooms, but there was a queue extending all the way round the tiny brick building. Somehow she didn't think Kelly Kay would wait in a queue just to hide.

There was really nowhere else left to look, and Mary was starting to get worried. Maybe something bad had happened to Kelly Kay. Here she was, all alone in a strange city, and she didn't know a single soul.

Mary Bubnik decided to circle the park once more. As she followed the path round the lake, something in the water caught her eye. It looked like a wisp of pink candyfloss wrapped round the rushes. Mary scrambled down the bank and reached into the ice-cold water.

Her hand closed round the thin pink fabric and Mary shivered. There, in the palm of her hand, was a familiar lace handkerchief with the initials KK monogrammed in one corner. And Mary knew who owned it.

"Kelly Kay!" Mary Bubnik cried out. "What if she fell in the lake? She can't swim. She could have . . ." Mary didn't even dare think the word *drowned*.

Instead she clutched the wet handkerchief to her chest and whispered, "I have got to get help." She ducked her head down and ran as fast as she could to find her friends.

Chapter Eleven

"It was really nice of you guys to quit the contest and help me," Mary Bubnik breathed as the gang followed her along the trail to the lake. "I know it meant a lot to you."

"Aw, it was nothing." Rocky showed Mary her empty Easter basket. "We were losing anyway."

"I'm just so worried that Kelly may have — " Mary gulped back a fresh wave of fear. "You know . . ."

"Drowned?" Gwen supplied the dreaded word.

Mary nodded slowly. "Uh-huh."

"Why do you think that?" Gwen asked. "Can't she swim?"

Mary Bubnik shook her head sadly. "She had

lessons every summer at the public pool but she could just never learn."

"I can't imagine not knowing how to swim." McGee was amazed. From June on she practically lived in the pool.

"Poor Kelly Kay," Mary Bubnik wailed. "It's all my fault. I let her go running off and now she could be out there." She pointed to the lake that shone an ominous black in the afternoon light. Mary squeezed her eyes shut and put her head in her hands. "It's too awful to think about."

"Then don't," Zan said, putting one hand on her shoulder. "Because I'm certain that Kelly Kay has not drowned."

Mary blinked her big blue eyes at Zan. "Why are you so sure about that?"

"Because that lake is very shallow. You'd have to swim out to the middle to drown. And she wouldn't go swimming if she didn't know how to swim," Zan reasoned.

"That makes sense," Mary Bubnik agreed.

"Especially not in her nice Easter dress," Zan added.

"That's true. She's become very concerned about her looks," Mary said thoughtfully, "Plus, the water is freezing. But what about her handkerchief?"

"Yeah, doesn't that mean something?" McGee wanted to know.

"It means that she did pass this way," Zan explained, looking off into the distance. "My guess is that she was probably heading for the woods, and most likely crying. Why else would someone use a hanky."

"*Crying?*" Mary Bubnik repeated in a hushed whisper. "That means she could be hurt!"

"Or depressed," Gwen considered. "Was she depressed about something, Mary?"

Mary winced. "Well, yes. We did have a fight on the way over here this morning."

"Try not to think about that now, Mary," Zan said gently. "Everything will work out OK."

Mary sighed shakily. "I hope so."

In silence, the four girls followed Zan down the path and into the woods.

After they had travelled a short way, the trail forked into two footpaths. The right path angled back round the edge of the lake. The one on the left disappeared into a thicket of tall bushes.

"Let's go right," Rocky suggested.

Hearing music coming from that direction, Mary nodded her head. "She probably went to the right 'cause that would take her back toward the band. I say we go to the right, too."

"No." Zan shook her head firmly. "In this case, right is wrong. I think she went to the left."

"Why?" Rocky asked, staring down the left path.

"It's just a dead end. There's nothing down there but an old stone wall."

"Anyone who's ever been to Deerfield Park knows that," McGee added.

"Not Kelly Kay," Gwen pointed out. "She's never been here before in her life."

"If it was me," McGee said, "I'd go where there was people and music and fun. To the right."

"Which is exactly why Kelly Kay went left," Zan countered. "If I was crying, I wouldn't want to be seen by a lot of people. I'd turn away from the noise."

"Zan's right," Mary Bubnik cried. "I'd do that, too."

"Let's go then," McGee said.

Zan took the lead along the left footpath, with the others following in single file behind her.

"I hope we find her soon," Gwen mumbled, "because I'm getting hungry." She had counted on finding lots of chocolate eggs at the Easter egg hunt and hadn't brought along her usual supply of snacks.

Suddenly Zan stopped and pointed straight ahead. "Look!"

Kelly Kay was sitting on a big boulder near the end of the path. When she heard the girls coming, she turned and faced the stone wall.

"Kelly Kay!" Mary Bubnik lunged forward and rushed to her friend's side. "Are you hurt?"

"No," Kelly Kay replied keeping her face away from them.

"We were so worried," Mary babbled. "We looked everywhere for you."

"Why didn't you show up for the hunt?" Rocky asked.

"I didn't feel like it." Kelly Kay kicked at the wall with her foot.

"Didn't *feel* like it?" Gwen raised her eyebrows and gave Kelly a sharp look. "But we needed you."

"I'm sure you did just fine without me," Kelly replied dully.

"No, we didn't do fine," Mary said. "We dropped out of the race to look for you."

At that moment the loudspeaker across the lake blared out: "And the winner of the Annual Easter Egg Hunt is ... the team from the Deerfield Academy of Dance."

"The Bunheads!" all five girls shrieked. "I don't believe it!"

Rocky flung her Easter basket down in the dirt and marched up to Kelly Kay. "And it's all your fault!"

Kelly kept staring at the wall. "So you lost the egg hunt," she said with a shrug. "Big deal."

McGee joined Rocky and shoved her face up close to Kelly Kay. "It was a *very* big deal."

Zan folded her arms across her chest. "We needed to win that hunt for our Academy."

Rocky slammed her fist into her palm. "And we wanted to beat the Bunheads!"

"Basically, we wanted to hunt for eggs, not for you," Gwen said, staring into her empty Easter basket.

Kelly Kay hung her head and her hair fell across her face. "Maybe I should never have come here."

"Maybe you shouldn't have," Rocky hissed.

"Maybe you should go back to Oklahoma," Gwen added.

"And your stupid ballet school in someone's stupid basement," McGee snapped.

The four girls surrounded Kelly Kay. Mary Bubnik couldn't believe what was happening. Her friends from Deerfield were being so mean, and she couldn't take it anymore. She shoved her way through their circle and stood beside Kelly Kay. "You stop yelling at her this minute," she demanded.

"She deserves it," Rocky shot back.

"No, she doesn't!" Mary put her hands on her hips. "I can't believe you would gang up on her. Four against one. How fair's that?"

"I can't believe you're sticking up for her," McGee said, shaking her head. "After all she's done to you."

"I don't care if the Bunheads did win the contest, and the Academy goes down the drain," Mary said defiantly. "Kelly Kay's still my friend, and you can't treat her like that!"

Before anyone could say a word, Mary pulled Kelly to her feet and said, "Come on, Kelly Kay. We're going home."

The gang stood in stunned silence as they watched Mary Bubnik and Kelly Kay disappear down the path into the trees. The girls had never had a fight like this before.

Finally Zan spoke. "How could something that started so wonderfully end up so badly?"

McGee scratched her head. "Yeah. This spring holiday was supposed to be a blast."

Gwen ticked off the events on her fingers. "We were going to meet Kelly Kay, win the Easter egg hunt, and save the Academy."

"Instead – " Rocky aimed a swift karate kick at the stone wall. "The Bunheads wiped us out, the Academy's up for grabs – "

"And we may have just lost Mary Bubnik as a friend," Zan murmured, staring down at her feet. "Forever."

"What a bummer," Rocky finished glumly.

No one said anything for a long time.

"Well, as I see it," Gwen said brightly, "there's only one thing we can do."

All eyes focused on her.

"What's that?" McGee asked.

"Go to Hi Lo's," Gwen replied, "and drown our troubles in a Super Dooper Easter Sundae with nuts, cherries, and a double dose of whipped cream."

"That might cheer us up," McGee said, forcing a smile.

"Yeah." Rocky picked up her Easter basket and dusted it off. "But I doubt it."

Chapter Twelve

Mary Bubnik stumbled blindly down the footpath, hot tears stinging her eyes. She felt as if her world had come to an end. Her friendship with Kelly Kay was over, and now, in one fell swoop, she'd lost all her new friends in Deerfield.

"Mary, wait!"

Mary could hear Kelly's feet pounding along behind her. She didn't want to stop. She wished she could keep running — away from Kelly Kay, away from Deerfield, away from everything.

Kelly caught up and grabbed Mary by the elbow. "Mary, please stop!"

Mary locked her knees. She was trying so hard to keep back tears when she turned to look at Kelly

104

Kay her face was contorted into a horrible frown. "What?"

Kelly Kay saw the look on her face, took a step back, and stammered, "I, uh, I just . . . that was real brave of you to stick up for me back there."

Mary shrugged. "You're my guest, and they were being mean." She tried to turn away but Kelly grabbed her shoulder again.

"I guess I just wanted to thank you."

Mary bit her lip, afraid to say anything.

Kelly took a deep breath. "I mean, I know I've been acting really rotten . . ."

"Yes, you have," Mary said, her chin quivering. "And I don't understand why." She stared hard at Kelly Kay, whose own face suddenly clouded over. Mary was stunned to see two big tears roll down cheeks.

"I don't know why," Kelly Kay said in a choked voice. "I've been looking forward to this visit for six whole months."

Mary nodded. "Me too."

"And — and then, when we finally got together, everything seemed to have changed."

"Well, sure, things had changed," Mary said. "But not between us." Suddenly the dam that had been holding back her own tears burst and she sobbed, "not until you got here. Why?"

"I don't know." Kelly suddenly threw her arms around Mary. "I'm just so sorry!"

The two girls stood in the middle of the path, crying and hugging each other. Finally Kelly sniffed loudly. She started to wipe her nose on her sleeve when Mary handed her the still-damp handkerchief that she'd found in the lake. Kelly took it and blew her nose. "Thanks."

"It's nothing." Mary wiped the tears away from her eyes with the back of her hand.

Kelly took another deep breath, and explained, "You see, ever since you left Oklahoma, I've been so lonely."

"You have?" Mary asked with a little hiccup. "But I thought you had such a great life out there."

Kelly stared at her handkerchief. "My life's been miserable. I don't have any friends – "

"What about Marla Huddleston?" Mary interrupted.

Kelly wrinkled her nose. "I can't stand her. Marla's still just as awful as you said. I made all that up."

Mary's eyes widened. "But why?"

"'Cause your life seemed to be so much better than mine." She picked mournfully at the lace handkerchief and said softly, "When I saw that you'd made all these new friends, I thought that you didn't need me anymore."

"I *do* need you!" Mary cried, her eyes filling with fresh tears.

"Well, it didn't seem like it," Kelly Kay replied. "I mean, you'd already made all these plans when I got here. I was just in the way."

"Look," Mary Bubnik squeezed her friend's hand gently, "I may have moved to a new place, and made some new friends, but you'll always be my very best friend in the whole wide world."

"I will?" Kelly Kay asked in a small voice.

"Of course." Mary draped her arm round her friend's shoulder. "I've told you secrets I've never told another living soul."

Kelly Kay managed a smile. "Me too."

Mary made a fist and jokingly waved it at Kelly Kay. "And if you tell anyone, I will personally walk back to Oklahoma and strangle you."

Kelly threw back her head and laughed. Mary joined in. It was the first time the girls had really giggled together since Kelly had arrived and it felt good.

Mary looped her arm through Kelly's and they walked back along the path toward the bandstand.

"You know, it was really hard for me when I first moved to Deerfield," Mary Bubnik confessed. "For the first time in my whole life, I didn't have any friends at all."

Kelly Kay looked at her in amazement. "Wow, really? You never mentioned that in your letters."

"I guess I didn't want to admit it," Mary said shyly.

"Mom enrolled me in anything she could, but I was a disaster at everything. Then she signed me up for *The Nutcracker* tryouts, and I met the gang. And we've been good friends ever since."

Kelly grimaced and said, "Until today."

Mary waved a hand, not wanting to think about the awful fight. She focused her big blue eyes on her friend intently. "But you can do the same thing," she declared. "I've got an idea. When you go home, pretend you've just moved to Oklahoma, and you're starting a whole new life. Talk to kids you think you'd like to have as friends and join some new clubs."

"D'you really think that would help?" Kelly Kay asked tentatively.

"Sure I do. It worked for me, and it can work for you." Mary beamed confidently at her friend. "Before long, you'll have more friends than you know what to do with."

Kelly Kay shrugged and said, "I'll try it!"

The two girls hugged each other, squashing their Easter baskets between them.

"Thanks for everything, Mary," Kelly whispered. "And I'm really sorry I acted so badly and said those mean things about Mr Toad. I know how you feel about him."

"That's OK."

"I'm especially sorry I made you guys lose the Easter egg hunt."

"Don't worry about it," Mary replied, her voice muffled against Kelly's shoulder. "I think the gang will get over it." She pulled back and whispered mischievously, "I never thought I'd say something like this, but I'm glad the Bunheads won. That means the Academy will get the thousand dollar prize."

Kelly Kay grinned at her old friend through a haze of tears. "You know, Mary Bubnik, I don't think you've changed one little bit."

"Neither have you, Kelly Kay Kingston," Mary cried. "And I'm so glad!" Her eyes widened suddenly and she said, "I've got a great idea! Let's go and celebrate staying best friends."

"Great!" Kelly Kay giggled and added, "Actually, I'm starved, if you want to know the truth."

"Come on, then!" Mary Bubnik cried, taking Kelly by the hand and hurrying down the footpath. "I know the perfect place to eat."

"Where?"

"My favourite restaurant in all of Deerfield," Mary replied. "Hi Lo's Pizza and Chinese Food To Go!"

Chapter Thirteen

Rocky, McGee, Zan, and Gwen were still upset about the fight with Mary Bubnik when they trudged into Hi Lo's place. He was sitting in the lone booth at the back of the restaurant, watching the television set that hung from a wall bracket.

"My friends! Have you seen the news?" Hi exclaimed. "You've been on all afternoon!"

"Us?" Gwen stared at him in disbelief. "Really?"

"That TV interview must've really paid off," Rocky cried, stripping off her jacket and flinging it onto an empty stool. "I knew it! Today local TV, tomorrow — Hollywood!"

The girls hurried over to join Hi in the booth.

"Maybe now the Academy truly can be saved," Zan sighed.

McGee nodded. "Yeah, all we need is some rich people to send some money *pronto*."

Hi Lo held his hands up in dismay. "But the news accounts haven't even mentioned the Ballet Academy. Just you."

"What do you mean?" Rocky asked.

Hi gestured at the television. "See for yourselves."

An advertisement ended and Bob Beasely's face filled the screen. He was seated behind a desk in the newsroom of the studio.

"Wow, it's really him!" Rocky exclaimed. "I can't believe it! He looks much better on TV."

"Be quiet," Gwen barked, "he's starting to talk."

The gang glued their eyes to the screen.

"Spring Fest in Deerfield is usually a time for celebration," the newsman intoned, "a time for families to enjoy the warm weather, their neighbours, and each other."

The screen shifted to a view of the crowds at the Spring Fest, milling around the booths and tables.

"But some of us aren't so lucky," Bob Beasely said. "Sometimes families get in trouble and need assistance. Channel 29's *We Care* programme has helped hundreds of families in Deerfield. We'd like to be able to do that again. Today we discovered five girls who found a dramatic way to ask for help."

111

Suddenly they saw themselves on the screen, marching up and down with their posters, chanting, "Save D.A.D.! Save D.A.D.!"

"Oh, wow!" Rocky cried. "We made it big time." She gave McGee's arm a squeeze.

"Wait a minute," Zan urged them. "Let's hear what Bob says."

"I found these girls crying desperately in the park," the reporter declared. "They were dressed in their Easter best but there was nothing happy about their message."

The camera cut to a close-up of Rocky clutching her stomach, then waving her poster and wailing, "Save D.A.D., please!"

"That was some great acting," McGee said, clapping Rocky on the back. "Those lessons at the base are really paying off."

"Yes, you were really wonderful," Zan agreed.

Rocky turned pink. "Thanks, guys."

"As far as we can tell, the girls' father is in trouble, and they are worried about being split up, and never being able to see one another again," the reporter said. "During the interview they handed out leaflets among the crowd of bystanders, asking for donations of support."

The screen zoomed in and showed one of their leaflets close up, then Bob's face came back on. "Unfortunately I had to leave them for a moment to get some more videotape," he explained. "And I never saw them again."

"We forgot all about him!" Gwen gasped.

"He must still have our posters," Zan said.

"Shhh!" McGee ordered, craning forward to hear the rest of the report. Everyone fell silent and listened intently.

"The girls also carried signs like this one." Bob held up one of the placards in front of the camera.

"That's mine!" Zan whispered excitedly.

"Shhh!" everyone hissed.

"Unfortunately we don't have a happy ending to report. But what we know is this." Bob stared directly into the camera and his voice took on a serious tone. "Somewhere in this city tonight, a father is in trouble. We don't know why, or where. But his brave daughters' poignant pleas for help will be of no use unless we can find them."

"What's he talking about?" Rocky exclaimed. The others stared at the screen in shock.

"On behalf of this station, I'm asking anyone with information regarding the whereabouts of these five girls to please call Channel 29 immediately. We care." A number flashed on the screen for a moment, and then the regular programming resumed. Hi flicked off the set with a remote control.

"He doesn't know that the Academy is D.A.D.," Zan muttered.

"He thinks we've lost our father." Gwen shook her head in amazement.

McGee swallowed hard. "*I* think we're in trouble."

The phone rang and Hi went into the kitchen to answer it. Moments later he stuck his head out of the door and called, "Rocky, it's for you. It's Sergeant Garcia."

Rocky's eyes grew huge as saucers. "Make that *big* trouble." She slid out of the booth and headed for the phone.

The little bell above the door tinkled, announcing the arrival of new customers. The girls turned to see who it was just as Mary Bubnik and Kelly Kay stepped through the door.

Nobody moved. Nobody said a word.

"Oh," Mary Bubnik said finally. "I didn't know you were all here."

She turned to go when McGee cried, "Wait! You can't leave. We need you."

Zan nodded. "Something dreadful has happened."

"And it's all my fault!" Kelly Kay burst out. "I'm so sorry!"

Gwen cocked her head in confusion. "What are you talking about?" Then she remembered their fight in the park. "Oh, forget about that. We've got bigger problems to deal with."

The girls quickly explained to Mary and Kelly the mix-up about "Save D.A.D.!"

"I suppose we should have written out our slogan," Mary said. "Then everyone would have known we meant the Academy."

Just then Rocky threw open the door from the kitchen and announced dramatically, "It's worse than we thought. The phone hasn't stopped ringing at my house since the first news bulletin. My father says the same thing is happening at your houses, too."

Everyone gasped at once. Meanwhile Rocky slipped on her red satin jacket over her dress.

"Where are you going?" Zan cried.

"Dad wants me home on the double – that means *now*!" Rocky sprinted for the door.

"You can't go yet!" McGee shouted. "We still have to work out what we're going to do."

"*Do*?" Rocky spun round and faced the gang. "I can't do anything," she thundered. "I've just been grounded for a month."

"Oh no," Mary Bubnik said.

"Dad's given me strict orders to call the station and tell them the truth."

Gwen stared at the others. "We're going to look like total idiots."

"You shouldn't do that," Kelly Kay blurted out.

Rocky, McGee, Gwen, and Zan turned and glared at her coldly but she ignored them.

115

"I think what's happened is the best publicity the Academy could ever get."

"You've got to be kidding!" Rocky spluttered.

"They need this kind of publicity like they need a hole in the head," Gwen scoffed.

"Wait a minute," Mary Bubnik cried. "Listen to Kelly Kay. She knows what she's talking about. Her dad works in public relations for a big oil company back – "

"We know," groaned Rocky, rolling her eyes. "Back in Oklahoma."

Kelly Kay sighed heavily. "I know you think I'm a jerk, and you wish I would just go away, but just hear me out for a second."

The gang crossed their arms and waited for Kelly Kay to speak.

"If Rocky tells the station it was just a big mix-up," Kelly said, "then the TV station will feel really dumb and drop the story. But if you let them keep thinking there are five girls still out there, trying to save their father – they'll want to put you on the air again."

"So we can make bigger fools of ourselves?" Gwen said sarcastically.

"No." Kelly Kay grinned slyly. "So you can explain what 'Save D.A.D.' *really* means." She looked from one girl to the next. "Think about it – thousands of people all over Deerfield will be watching, ready to help."

116

"What a brilliant idea!" Hi exclaimed from behind the counter. All of the girls turned to look at him in surprise. "I think you should call Channel 29 right now, and tell them you're the girls they're looking for. And that you've got something very important to say on the air."

The girls gulped. "Now?"

"Yes," Hi insisted, clapping his hands together. "Strike while your news is hot."

Rocky faced the group and asked, "OK, who wants to make the call?"

"Not me," Gwen and McGee said at the same time.

Mary Bubnik giggled. "I'd probably say all the wrong things."

"And I'd completely freeze under all that pressure," Zan said hurriedly.

Rocky put her hands on her hips. "Why do I always have to be the one to do the hard things? You guys are all a bunch of chickens."

"Who are you calling a chicken?" McGee retorted.

It looked as if they were about to start fighting among themselves again when Kelly Kay realized that this was her opportunity to patch things up with the gang. "I'll make the call," she declared.

"You will?" The girls gaped at her in amazement.

"Sure," Kelly replied with a grin. "I'll just pretend I'm one of you."

McGee breathed a huge sigh of relief. "Kelly, that is great!"

"Fabulous!" Gwen agreed.

Mary Bubnik wrapped her arm around Kelly's shoulder proudly. "That's my friend!"

Kelly Kay's face turned a vivid pink and she stared shyly at the floor. "It's the least I can do," she mumbled, "after all the trouble I've caused." She lifted her head and asked, "Where's the phone?"

"Over here." Hi leaned over the counter with the receiver in his hand. "I've already called Channel 29 and they're ready to talk."

Kelly Kay squared her shoulders, then marched up to the counter and took the receiver from Hi Lo. "Hello, I'm one of the girls you're looking for," she said proudly. "The one who's D.A.D. needs saving." Kelly turned and winked at the gang. "I'd like to talk to Bob Beasely — your head reporter."

Chapter Fourteen

When the girls arrived at the television station several people were already in the lobby waiting to meet them.

A short, bald-headed man with glasses stepped forward to shake their hands. "I'm Gus Targett, the *We Care* segment producer. Boy, am I glad to see you!" He gestured to a girl with flaming red hair dressed in a mini-skirt and lots of jewelry. "This is Coco. She'll be doing your make-up."

"Make-up?" Gwen repeated. "What for?"

"Because we go on the air in — " The man named Gus checked his watch. "Fifteen minutes."

He herded the girls out of the lobby and down a long corridor to the make-up room, where they

119

were placed in front of big lighted mirrors. Coco and her two assistants crowded round them, applying eye-liners, powders and rouge.

Kelly Kay hung back in the doorway and watched.

"Come on, Kelly," Mary Bubnik called as Coco tried to apply lipstick to her moving mouth. "I think you should be on TV, too."

"Yeah! The more the merrier," McGee said as a short round girl combed her hair and re-plaited it.

"We need you, Kelly." Zan paused while a man in jeans and a canvas jacket clipped a microphone to the lapel of her blouse, then added dramatically, "D.A.D. needs you!"

Kelly's face lit up as she allowed herself to be seated by a make-up artist. "Wait till the kids in Oklahoma find out I was on TV! Boy, will they be impressed!"

Within minutes they were all made-up and wired for sound. Then the producer appeared in the doorway.

"OK, girls," Gus Targett announced, "it's showtime!"

He hustled them out of the make-up room and down the hall, talking non-stop. The girls had to run to keep up with him. "You're going to be interviewed by Linda Lawrence, the evening anchor for Channel 29. Now she'll tell you exactly what to do. Just listen carefully, OK?" Gus pushed open a pair of thick metal doors and ushered them into the studio. "Here we are."

An assistant led the girls to a row of chairs positioned on the newsroom set. "Now sit down, and sit still," the woman ordered.

"I wish I'd been allowed to bring my chocolate eggs with me," Gwen moaned. "I'm so nervous."

"I don't think they want to interview people with their mouths full," Rocky said.

A few minutes later a woman dressed in an apricot-coloured suit stepped onto the set. She was very tall and very slender, and her straight blonde hair hung stylishly down above her serious grey eyes. As she took a seat across from the girls, the woman smiled warmly at the girls. "I'm Linda Lawrence," she said, clipping a microphone to her lapel. "You may have seen me on the news before."

"I have!" Mary Bubnik cried, her curls bouncing with excitement.

Rocky stared at the celebrity with admiration. "Wow. You look even better in person."

Linda smiled. "Thank you. Now I'll be asking you a few questions. And when you answer, make sure you look directly into the lens of the camera."

Gwen stared at the three cameras positioned on the floor. "Which one?"

"Whichever one has the little red light on," Linda instructed.

"Sounds easy," Gwen said, pressing her sweaty palms against her dress.

The floor manager moved to the edge of the set and announced, "OK, we're giving you a ten second countdown, and then you're on the air."

Mary Bubnik gasped. "Ten seconds!"

The girls sat frozen in their chairs, staring at the cameras and waiting for the red light to come on.

"Ten, nine, eight, seven, six, five, four, three, two, and go!" The floor manager gestured at the announcer, who faced the center camera just as its red light blinked on.

"Good evening," she said in a firm voice. "I'm Linda Lawrence, and welcome to the weekend edition of Channel 29's Action News."

Linda shifted her position slightly and looked into the left hand camera, which now had its red light on. "We begin this report with our *We Care* segment. This story started earlier today at the Deerfield Spring Fest."

Rocky nudged McGee with her elbow and pointed at the monitor overhead. The girls were plainly visible on the screen.

"Oh, now, I look huge," Gwen muttered disconsolately.

"The camera always adds fifteen pounds to you," Rocky whispered.

Gwen's eyes widened in alarm. "Permanently?"

122

Rocky didn't have time to explain for just then Linda Lawrence turned to the girls and said, "All of us here at the studio are so glad you consented to be with us this evening. We have a lot of questions about the father" – she glanced at Zan and cleared her throat – "um, or fathers, of you five."

Linda paused for a second and surveyed the six girls sitting on the stage in front of her. "I suppose I should say, *six* girls. Your number seems to be growing – "

"Excuse me, Ms Lawrence," McGee interrupted, "but we came on TV here tonight because we want to straighten out a misunderstanding."

The announcer looked a bit taken aback. "Please do."

McGee looked for the camera with the red light on and took a deep breath. "All of our dads are fine and don't need saving. I mean, we all have different fathers, you see, and we're not related to each other at all."

Rocky sat bolt upright as she remembered that she was supposed to have been at home an hour ago. Her father was probably ready to call out the National Guard to find her. She leaned into the picture and added, "I personally would like to mention *my* dad, Master Sergeant Richard Garcia of the United States Air Force, who is really the greatest, most understanding dad in the world." She aimed her most winning smile right into the lens, then slumped back in her chair. "And he'll probably ground me for the rest of my life for being on this show," Rocky muttered under her breath.

"Save D.A.D. means, Save the Deerfield Academy of Dance," McGee explained. "That's our ballet school."

Linda Lawrence's eyes widened in shock. "So, girls, let me get this straight." She folded her hands across her notepad and leaned forward. "What you're saying is that your D.A.D. is *really* a ballet school, and not a real *dad*?"

"That's right," Gwen said. "We went to the Spring Fest to let everybody know about the trouble the Academy is in."

"And to get people to help by giving donations," Rocky added.

"You see, the building is going to be sold to someone else," Zan explained, "unless we can raise enough money to buy it for the Academy."

Linda Lawrence raised an eyebrow. "So the Academy told its own students to go out and beg for money?"

"No!" McGee exclaimed. "This was all our idea."

"We just wanted to help the best way we could," Zan explained.

"So we tried to come up with a really cool way of raising money *fast*," Rocky said proudly. Then she frowned and added, "At least, it seemed a cool idea at the time."

"If we don't raise enough money," Mary Bubnik went on, "the Academy will go out of business." She looked at the gang and added, "The Academy means a lot to us because we all go to different schools, and our dance classes are the only time we have to see each other."

"And we all intend to become great ballerinas some day," Kelly Kay said suddenly.

The other girls stared at her curiously. Obviously, Kelly Kay didn't realize that they *hated* ballet!

"Well, we do," she persisted. "Don't we?"

The girls looked at each other and shrugged helplessly.

"Yes!" they chorused. "We *love* ballet!"

"But if the Academy closes," Zan said seriously, "a lot of promising ballet careers will be over. And a lot of truly dedicated people will lose their jobs, like Miss Delacorte, the receptionist – "

"And Miss Springer, our teacher," Mary Bubnik cut in.

"Not to mention, Mr Anton and Miss Jo, the directors," Gwen pointed out.

McGee turned and faced the camera squarely. "So, please, everybody, if you care about ballet – help save D.A.D.!"

"That is, the Deerfield Academy of Dance," Rocky

said quickly, just in case someone had tuned in late and thought they meant "dad" again.

"Well!" Linda Lawrence paused for a moment, a tight smile on her face. "This is *quite* a story." She turned back to the camera. "We're going to take a short break, but I'll be right back after this word from our sponsor."

Linda smiled warmly at the camera until the little red light blinked off. Then she stood up abruptly and her clipboard clattered to the floor. "Gus!" she bellowed. "I want an explanation right now!"

"Be right there," he shouted from the back of the studio.

As he wove his way through the cameras, Linda spluttered, "I can't believe it! This is all you could find for our *We Care* Programme? Five – " she shot a stern look at Kelly Kay – "or should I say, *six* girls wanting to stay in the same ballet class. Who's going to care about that?"

"Judging by our audience response, lots of people." Gus rushed forward with a glass of water. "Now, Linda, try to stay calm."

Linda looked confused. "What are you talking about?"

"The switchboard is lit up like a Christmas tree," Gus explained. "People are calling in from all over the state, wanting to know where to send their money to help the Academy."

Linda took a deep sip of water. "You've got to be joking."

"Listen, we're cutting back on the rest of the local news items tonight and sticking with the girls," Gus went on. "The viewers love 'em!"

"Did you hear that?" McGee whispered. "They love us!"

"Five seconds," the floor manager called.

"Now pick up the human interest angle," Gus shouted to Linda, "and run with it."

The announcer nodded and took her seat again just as the red light went on.

"Welcome back to *We Care*," she said. "We have six remarkable young ladies from the Deerfield Academy of Dance with us tonight. And, from the hundreds of calls that have poured in to our switch-board, I can see that all of you watching at home are as impressed as I am by the girls' ingenuity, imagination, and most important, their deep commitment to a cause they care about – preserving one of Deerfield's cultural treasures and – "

Suddenly a man slipped up beside Linda Lawrence and handed her a folded piece of paper. She read it quickly and her eyes grew as huge as saucers.

"Ladies and gentlemen," the announcer declared, looking back into the camera, "I have a wonderful announcement to share with you. It appears that our little fund-raisers have succeeded beyond their wildest dreams. A local benefactor — who insists on remaining anonymous — has decided to purchase Hillberry Hall, the present home of the Academy, and present it as a gift to the ballet company."

"Did you hear that?" McGee cried, leaping to her feet. "We did it! We saved D.A.D.!"

"All *right!*" Rocky bellowed, giving McGee a thump on the shoulder. The rest of the girls threw their arms around Rocky and McGee. They hopped up and down in a circle, screaming "Yea!" at the top of their lungs.

"This is fantastic!" Gwen exclaimed.

"Now that they own the building," Zan cried, "the Academy will never have money troubles again!"

"*And* — " Mary Bubnik grabbed Kelly Kay by the hand and leaped into the center of the huddle. "Now we can take ballet for the rest of our lives!"

"The rest of our lives?" The others froze in their tracks and slowly turned to face the camera. "Oh, *no!*"